EXTREME TEMPERATURES

CHASE MCPHERSON

© 2025 Chase McPherson

This is a work of fiction. Names, characters, businesses, places, events, locales, and incidents are either the products of the author's imagination or used in a fictitious manner. Any resemblance to actual persons, living or dead, or actual events is purely coincidental.

This story contains veiled as well as overt references to attempted suicide and self-harm. Please use discretion when reading. If you or someone you know is dealing with these issues, please seek help from your local or national mental health advocacy services.

Other titles in the *Bloodbound* series:
Reawakening
West of Nowhere
Alternate Tracks

For anyone who ever struggled to figure out their place in the world, to find their tribe, or who fought through it all to discover more about themselves.

1
RUNNING HOT

Slicer's looked out-of-place in every sense of the word. For starters, the sign spelling out the name of the dive bar was a hodgepodge - each letter came from one of the signs that had hung over the threshold during other businesses' brief time in operation at that location. The desired letter had been sheared, torn, or indeed sliced off, then glued, cemented, or soldered to the next. The finished sign, which looked like it came from a ransom note you'd see in the movies, was riveted to the corrugated metal walls of the building.

The building – a half-moon shaped, forest green quonset hut - was a disused military barracks, the only building left from a closed base. It stood in stark contrast from the shopping center on the opposite side of the interstate. The bar was isolated, cut off from the main artery of interstate highway traffic, serviced only by a gravelly side road, and surrounded by pastures and crop fields.

Slicer's parking lot also was markedly different – again, also paved with loose gravel, and guardrails made out of treated logs. And there was not a sedan or a family-packed van to be found. There were, however, plenty of motorcycles. Dozens of them. Shiny, buffed Harleys; dust-covered Kawasakis; and more than a few Hondas in various conditions. Lights from the lamps surrounding the building danced across chrome. And within this lot full of hogs, there was one vehicle that itself stood out from the rest - a three-wheeled Can-Am, plastic armor coated in Day-Glo green with accents of construction-site orange. It was parked around the corner from the rest of the bikes, against an otherwise desolate alleyway leading to the rear pasture.

A pair of men were pointing at the trike, kicking its tires and sniggering. One of them walked around to the rear tire. The license plate above it read HUNTR. The sound of a zipper being undone was masked by the pair of men hooting in glee, while a stream of yellow liquid began to splatter against the plate.

Meanwhile, inside the metallic shell of a building, your typical biker bar activities: drinking, shouting, loud music, pool-playing. There were a few women inside, including one tending bar, but the place was decidedly testosterone-filled. As with everything else about its exterior, at least one thing inside the bar was out of place for the setting – the tattoo chair in the back room, only half-concealed by a pool table and the four men shooting a game around it.

Two things were out of place, actually, if you counted the man being tattooed on the chair. Whereas most of the patrons of the bar were obviously of a certain breed, with scraggly beards, scratched and scuffed leather vests, and blue denim jeans, the young man in the chair was clean-shaven, with sandy blond hair, and was wearing tan cargo pants with a fabric belt tied around his waist. His left arm was propped up on the leather rest while the tattoo artist continued filling in a tribal design in rusty-red ink. The pattern was being snaked around the shoulder from its starting point at the man's left pectoral muscle.

The artist lifted his head to swipe a lock of salt-and-pepper hair behind his ear. He had a thick stubble around his chin and steely gunmetal blue eyes that took an examination of his work thus far. "Alright," he said, "I guess I *was* wrong. This is gonna be a five-draw job instead of four. I need another needle. Can you behave yourself while I get it, Hunter?"

"Told ya it'd be five," smirked Hunter, flexing his arm. Only a person watching very closely would notice the marks caused by the tattoo needle's piercing of his skin were healing, fully, by the second. "Go on, get your supplies. I'll be here."

The tattoo artist removed his black latex gloves, lifted himself off his stool, and headed for a room marked 'OFFICE.' Before entering, he snapped his fingers in Hunter's direction, and the young man looked his way. Pointing to his lips, the artist mouthed the word, "Behave!" Hunter replied with a playfully sarcastic face and a casual flip of his left hand's middle finger.

Leaning back in the chair, Hunter sighed and waited, looking out upon the back room, and watched the quad of pool players finish up their game, only to insert more quarters to call back the set of balls. Among the sounds of inane chatter, billiard balls clinking and being reracked, Hunter also noticed a pair of voices from the front of the house – loud, obnoxious voices. One was very talkative, while the other seemed overwhelmed by laughter.

"Whose is it – is it yours?"

"Fuck off," came the reply.

"Heheheheheheeeee!" A feral snort punctuated the drunken laugh. This voice was different from the first. But Hunter could tell he was the first voice's buddy.

"How bout you? You own that pussy bike outside?"

"Haaa..." Another drunken, horse-like snort.

"The hell are you talkin' bout – get outta here..."

Hunter rolled his eyes. Another drunk asshole, he thought to himself. Well, if it's all you can get...

Two men stumbled into the back room. One was short and squat, the other about a head taller and muscular.

"What about it?!" The muscular one scanned an obviously drunken eye around the room. "Who owns that so-called *motorcycle* outside? What fuckin' poser was so ashamed of it they parked it round back?"

The fat one let out a hyena-like snicker.

Hunter lifted himself out of the reclined position of the chair and smiled. "You mean the pussy bike?"

The musclehead was clearly soused, if not also high. There were wet stains on his shirt that indicated he'd had trouble keeping his last drink fully in his mouth. "Yeah, that's right," he sneered.

"Well, that'd be mine," Hunter said, his voice not displaying an ounce of fear or hesitation. "Why – you wanna take a ride with me?" There were muted snickers from the pool players. Hunter could feel the energy coming off everyone around. He was getting off on having an audience – but his next move, when he made it, had to be in private. Hunter hopped off the tattoo bench. He was about three inches shorter than the roughneck who was mouthing off to him.

"Boy, I'll fuck you *up*," the meathead growled. He cracked his knuckles, both hands balling into fists. His words were accentuated by his friend's hysterical laughter.

"Hm. Tempting, but I'm spoken for," Hunter cracked, which made the smaller of the pair belt out in laughter again. With a cross expression, the taller of the two smacked an arm to shut his pal up. "What'd you say, you little fagboy?"

"I said, if we're gonna dance, we're gonna take it over to *my* ballroom." Hunter began walking backwards, towards the exit. He kicked a leather-booted foot against the door, sending it sailing open. He bowed courteously and gestured outside with a swoop of his hand. "Won't you join me... Peaches?"

There were surprised 'ooohs,' hoots and cackles from the bikers watching the exchange, and as the pair began following Hunter outside, the office door opened, and the tattoo artist's arm grabbed for the shorter of the two. He yanked the man into the office, seemingly going unnoticed by Hunter or his 'dance partner.'

"Whoa," the tattooer said as he slammed the office door closed, holding up an arm and blocking a few of the bar patrons who approached the exit. "You know the rules – outdoor fights are invite only."

Hunter stepped out into the night, the cool air brushing against his bare chest like a whispered invitation. The gravel crunched beneath his boots as he moved toward the open field, his heightened senses already picking up the biker's erratic heartbeat. He smirked to himself, his tongue grazing the sharp points of his fangs, which were eagerly waiting to pop out fully. The scent of sweat and stale beer wafted from the man stumbling behind him.

This would be quick. It always was.

"Let's do this," the muscled biker said once he and Hunter made their way to the edge of the pasture behind the bar, thumbing his nose and getting into a boxer's stance.

This time, it was Hunter who cracked a laugh.

"What's so fuckin' funny?" growled the man.

"What is this, Chicago in the '20s?" Hunter folded his arms against his bare chest. "If you're gonna hit me, fucking *hit me*, Sweet Pea. Look, I'll even let you throw the first punch" –

Without a moment's hesitation, a closed fist socked Hunter square in the jaw, throwing his head violently backwards. A few drops of blood splattered on the gravel below. His head still thrown back, Hunter chuckled, then made a spitting sound.

Two teeth clattered to the ground, along with a small pool of spittle and blood.

Hunter was still laughing, even as his assailant cracked his neck again and began bobbing back and forth, waiting for a counterpunch.

"Oh, now, this isn't fair," Hunter said, his tone still playful, even mirthful. The blood seeping from his mouth dribbled down like a disturbed clown who opted for a bright red frowning face instead of a smile.

"Figured a pussyboy like you wouldn't like a real fight," the drunken biker said.

"Oh, I *like* a fight." Hunter's voice went suddenly deeper, more menacing. As he pulled his head forward, he smiled wide, revealing the gaps in his teeth. The holes were filling in with new teeth, growing and lengthening in seconds – but they didn't stop at the same length as his other teeth. They were forming points and descending – becoming fangs.

The man in front of Hunter recoiled. "What the...?"

"I meant this isn't fair... for *you*." As Hunter spoke, his eyes began to glow as red as embers. "Now, remind me... who's gonna fuck *who* up?"

"Shit!" Thoroughly startled, the man began to scramble backwards, then turned tail and made a full-on escape toward the wheat field behind the bar. He quickly disappeared among the crops.

Hunter took off running, his boots crunching against the gravel before he plunged into the wheat field. The night swallowed him and his prey whole, the air thick with the scent of soil and ripe grain. The biker's labored breaths and frantic footfalls echoed in Hunter's hyper-aware mind, each sound amplifying his hunger.

The man gasped, his voice catching in his throat as he stumbled over a root, barely catching himself. The wheat whipped against his face, leaving faint red lines on his exposed skin. Every step seemed heavier, as though the field itself conspired to slow him down.

Hunter darted through the stalks like a wraith, silent and deadly. His lips parted in a grin that revealed the growing sharpness of his fangs. When he finally closed the gap, he didn't hesitate. With a predator's grace, he lunged.

The force of his tackle drove the biker to the ground, the man's face slamming into the dirt with a muffled cry. Hunter's fingers clamped around his shoulders, pinning him with unnatural strength.

"No–please–" the biker began, but his voice cut off in a strangled scream as Hunter wrenched his head to the side, exposing the pulsing vein of his neck.

The first bite was electric. Hot, coppery blood surged into Hunter's mouth, and his entire body shuddered with a rush of vitality. He growled low and guttural, his grip tightening as the biker thrashed beneath him.

The man's screams turned to wet, choking sobs. His hands clawed at the ground, pulling up handfuls of wheat and dirt in a desperate attempt to escape. His heart raced in wild panic, each beat fueling Hunter's feast.

I could kill you, Hunter thought. *This feels so damn good... I wonder what it would feel like to kill you just because I know I can?*

"By the way," he said aloud as he took a quick break from drinking the biker's blood, "don't think I couldn't hear you pissing on my bike. You're gonna clean it up... with your *tongue*."

He barely had time to process the fact that there was a sound akin to a canine growling coming rapidly from behind him before Hunter was tackled, the force of four paws jump-kicking off his sides sending him rolling to the ground.

The biker gasped and groaned in pain, fumbling forward on his hands and knees. Hunter, dazed, rolled onto his back to find a gray-and-black coyote in front of him, panting and baring its fangs. Then, as it began to stand on its hind legs, the coyote began to grow in size, stretching, as fur began to disappear, replaced by a human form. As it fully transformed, Hunter sat up and sighed. "Slicer, you're such a spoilsport. You know it's been three days since I last fed."

"Yeah," Slicer said, wiping his lock of hair back behind his ear. "Well, I told you to behave yourself. Glad to see you lasted a full 30 seconds this time."

"The *fuck*...?" The biker's voice was haggard and shaken. He was almost crab-walking along the ground, holding one hand against his bleeding neck.

Hunter flew forward, pinning the biker to the ground. His eyes, now glowing an amber, yellow hue, bored into the biker as he focused his attention. "Playtime's over, sugar," he whispered into the biker's ear with a disturbed smile of glee. "Time for you to run along home." Hunter stood up, towering over the man.

As if in a hypnotic trance, the man stood up. His eyes were also glowing yellow. "Run along home," he echoed, almost in a whisper.

"Oh. Almost forgot." Licking his thumb, Hunter pierced the skin with a fang, a droplet of blood forming. He gave it a quick smear over the bite marks on his victim's neck. The wounds zipped themselves closed in seconds. "Scoot," he said, pushing the man in the chest.

The man, stupefied, staggered his way out of the wheat field, back towards the bar.

"Alright you," Slicer said, "back inside. We've gotta finish up your tat, then I'm sending you back home. You know my rule - once you get in a fight, you're done for the night.'

"Yeah, yeah."

Slicer guided Hunter back out of the field. As they walked back to the bar's back door, Slicer said, "By the way, I can smell that guy's piss real strong coming off your Spyder - Might wanna hose that off."

"If you'd left me with him like I wanted, I was gonna have that taken care of."

The hum of the Can-Am's engine vibrated through Hunter's body, almost in sync with the lingering euphoria coursing through him. The neon lights of passing towns flickered like ghosts in the distance, their glow softened by the darkness of the open road.

As the city skyline came into view, he let out a long breath, the thrill of the hunt fading into the more familiar rhythm of his life. Feeding always left him wired, but tonight there was an edge to it–something about the fight, the chase, that had set his instincts aflame.

After the usual hour's ride back to Dallas, plus a brief detour through the nearest car wash, Hunter biked back to a downtown high-rise, parked in the underground garage, and hailed the elevator, impatiently pressing the call button. He was so full of energy, he felt as if he could easily scale the outer facade to get to the apartment.

The elevator car finally arrived and Hunter hopped in. Just as he pressed the button for the 20th floor penthouse, his phone buzzed.

"Hi," he said into the device cheerfully. "I just got in; I'm on my way up."

"I know, I could smell you as you pulled in," said the deep, seductively oily voice on the other end. It wasn't meant as a dig; Hunter and Gibson were able to easily sense each other's proximity by their heightened olfactory sense. "And, honey... you reek. Please take a shower before you settle in."

"Yes, dear," Hunter replied, mockingly, as the elevator halted on the top floor. He terminated the call as the doors opened up to a private corridor, and he strolled casually to the door, which was flanked by two security guards of identical height, weight, and appearance – right down to the faces. As he approached the guards, Hunter took a lapel from his sleeveless shirt and sniffed it. He had to admit, there was a certain funk to it. "Mick," he said. "Mack."

"Evening, Hunter," they said in perfect unison. "Welcome back." Mick craned his head outward, monitoring, while Mack unlocked the door to the suite and opened it for Hunter to pass.

Hunter strode in, taking his cycle keys, phone, and wallet out of his cargo pants, setting the items on a credenza beside the door. He closed the door behind him and looked around the dazzling, ultra-modern, bright-white apartment.

"Living rough again, I take it?" The voice coming from the back bedroom was silken and sultry, deep and avuncular. Gibson, Hunter's lover, always used that tone when welcoming him back. It was their regular thing.

"Yeah, got in a little scrape for my meal tonight," Hunter said. "But I should be good for at least a week."

"I'll get your shower going," Gibson called.

"Thanks."

Hunter heard the shower sputter to life, and as he pulled off his shirt, he turned to the mirror over the credenza, admiring the intricate body art now etched permanently into his body. He traced his fingers along the path of the design. He paused to give his nipple a quick, firm pinch.

"Care to join me in the shower?" Hunter shouted.

"Tempting offer," Gibson said, his voice coming nearer to Hunter. "I suppose I could take a few minutes to... what in the *hell* did you do?"

Hunter whirled around to face Gibson, whose face was tightened in anger.

"Is that... is that a *coyote's blood* tattoo?"

2
FEVER PITCH

"My God, what have you *done* to yourself?" Gibson sounded, to Hunter, like an overprotective mother freaking out over her daughter's first ear piercing. "You've lost your identity!"

"I have *not*," Hunter said, only barely aware he was sounding much like the rebellious daughter he just imagined. "I've always wanted a tat – I just never got the chance to before I was turned."

Gibson shook his head slowly from side to side, mouth agape. "I can't believe you did that," he said. "Do you have any idea what this means?"

"Well, it's sort of based on a tribal tat I saw in a magazine a few weeks ago, plus a few rune symbols."

Rolling his eyes, Gibson hissed, "Not the *design*, Hunter. The ink. Coyote blood."

"Yeah, ink infused with coyote blood is the only way the ink will stay in vampire skin. Slicer explained it to me," Hunter said. Smiling coyly, he ran a fingertip over a curl in the tribal design that encircled his left nipple. "Does this not look... hot?"

Gibson's stern look was the only response. Unfazed, Hunter breezed past his partner and continued on to the bathroom.

Following behind, Gibson continued his lecture. "Hotness notwithstanding, what do you know about that blood? Whose is it, for starters?"

"It's Slicer's. Jesus," Hunter said, disrobing entirely and stepping quickly into the shower. "You think I'd use just anyone's blood? He's an Order operative, I've been embedded with him for three months, and I trust him fully." Hunter cranked the water on. Steam began fogging the glass almost immediately as the piping-hot water glistened over Hunter's body.

"Fair enough," said Gibson, standing behind the sliding glass door, arms folded crossly. "But do you know the physiological ramifications of what you've done? It's his blood and your body – as a supernatural being, he'll be able to track you now, just like I can. Just like" –

"Yes, I am fully aware that he can track me!" Hunter's voice rose, both to counter the splatter of the shower water, and because of his growing hostility. "So can his pack mates. He and I discussed this for a full week before I finally decided to get it done. I *am* aware of what having his blood in my system means. Even being housed just under my skin, with his blood in me, he can sense my proximity and my location. But not to the same degree as you or..." He paused as he thought about Kai. "...or anyone else."

Hunter turned to face Gibson through the glass. He used a hand to wipe some of the condensation away so he could look Gibson in the eyes. "If he's part of the organization, I should imagine it wouldn't hurt to have another set of bodies who can help me out if I ever get into trouble."

"Yes. On the subject of trouble," Gibson said, nonchalantly removing the white chenille bathrobe hanging delicately from his slender shoulders. He stood there, nude, as he continued. "I felt the punch to the mouth you took earlier. I imagine Kai did too."

"I don't want to hear his name," Hunter spat, coldly. He slid the door open to allow Gibson to step inside.

"Fine." Gibson grabbed a loofah hanging from the back wall and handed it to Hunter. "My point: Getting into fights is not part of your mission - and neither is feeding from the patrons at that motorcycle bar."

"You're the one who encourages me to feed from live humans," Hunter protested, squeezing some liquid soap into the loofah and getting it sudsy. "'Stay attuned to my vampire nature,' I believe were your words?"

"Separate from the mission," Gibson clarified. "You're supposed to be gathering intel about this... smuggling operation, or whatever. Which leads me to my next item of business, and I'm sorry, I have to mention" –

"No!" Hunter held up both hands, the loofah landing on the floor with a sodden *thud*. "I know what you're gonna say - I have to speak with him. And I will. *Tomorrow*. Not tonight. Can I just have tonight without thinking about or saying his name?!"

"Fine," Gibson sighed. "Tomorrow."

Hunter leaned backward underneath the shower, the water cascading over his neck and chest. The tattoo, aided by his quick-acting vampire blood, was completely healed. "Now, c'mon," he said. "Despite the shock of seeing it for the first time... despite the fact it's laced with coyote blood... What do you think of it?"

Gibson stepped forward, allowing the water to begin flowing against his body. He placed a hand over Hunter's chest, examining the artwork, his fingertips going over the dark crimson ink.

"It is... extremely hot on you," Gibson admitted.

Smirking, Hunter pulled Gibson towards him for an elongated kiss under the steaming-hot water.

As dusk fell over the Dallas-Fort Worth Metroplex the next evening, Gibson drove Hunter to headquarters, rather than have Hunter take his trike. The building, once belonging to a large television station, had been gutted from the inside to house the inner workings of The Order's regional office. Nobody from the public suspected that this otherwise vacant-looking building was packed to the gills with security personnel and hundreds of investigators, researchers, tactical planners, and even trained killers.

"They've given me an office," Gibson mentioned as he drove his silver Corvette into what looked like a truck loading dock. The metallic door lifted, and Gibson drove forward into a winding maze of corridors leading to a secret underground parking deck.

"That's nice," Hunter said, earnestly, though he was distracted with the various threads lining the frayed fringe of his shirt. He had torn the sleeves off to turn it into more of a vest akin to the wardrobe of a biker, showing off his white undershirt as well as his new tattoos.

"Why?"

"I think they're going to put me in charge of the digital conversion of the archives," Gibson replied. "You know, since you.. resigned the post."

"Ah. And is that why I've been called to the principal's office?" Hunter's tone had again slipped into the sarcastic.

"No, Calhoun didn't tell me why they needed to see you," Gibson said with a sigh, finding his designated parking spot and pulling the convertible expertly, perfectly, in between the lines. Gripping the steering wheel, he took a deep, though unnecessary, breath. He needed to choose his words carefully, Gibson decided, and thought he'd begin with Hunter's pet name.

"Young one, would you please not speak to me that way? I'm not the one you're mad at in the third place. This whole... attitude change that's been going on the last few months is starting to disrupt both work and our home life in the second place, and you should really ease up on Kai because he didn't know this Duncan person was *your* father when he killed him in the first place."

Hunter closed his eyes and remembered the vibration he felt course through his body when he remembered how he found out: Transcribing old audio tapes of Kai's reports of previous cases, Hunter happened upon a recording detailing a disturbance at a West Texas shopping mall in the mid-80s. A man, an innocent bystander, had been mortally wounded in the melee. Kai, acting out of mercy, ended the man's life to prevent further suffering.

It turned out, during Kai's reconnaissance work after the incident, that the man's identity was revealed to be Duncan Reeves – a name Hunter knew to be that of his father. Hunter was only a few months old at the time of Duncan's death, meaning that Hunter had been robbed of the chance of ever getting to know his father.

Hunter rewound the tape and played the sound of Kai dictating the name 'Duncan Reeves' over and over for nearly an hour. The rest of that evening was a blur in Hunter's memory, except for a blazing, one-sided row at the home the two shared, and Hunter hurling a slew of profanities in Kai's direction. He stormed out of the house that night and hadn't been back in more than three months.

Hunter blinked as he snapped out of his trance and stared at Gibson. Gibson's eyes, normally tan, had glazed over in a bright emerald light, indicating deep-rooted concern and sincerity. It didn't happen often, at least with Gibson, so if he was doing it, Hunter knew this was coming from the heart. However, the anger still stirring in his stomach continued to fuel his behavior and his responses.

"So I should just… forget it? Is that what you're suggesting to me?" As he said the words, he felt a heat rising, radiating through his skin. He'd been feeling sensations like fire, boiling water, or just plain heat several times a day for weeks now. They intensified anytime he felt irritated, angry, or even mildly inconvenienced, such as just after their erotic shower the night before, when the bottle cap flew off the top of his ready-to-drink blood, staining the pajamas he'd put on.

"I'm suggesting you put it in the proper perspective," Gibson retorted. "Kai did not do it as a slight against *you*. He didn't know you existed back then. You and I have both read the file over and over again. It was a mercy killing. Yes, it robbed you of getting to know the man and having a proper father figure in your life. But it was an unintended consequence, weighted against the threat that would have faced society as a whole."

Hunter felt a throbbing in his head. Just like everything else, it seemed, the headache felt *hot*. He grunted and leaned his head against the passenger window.

Gibson pressed a button; the window began to roll down. "No leaving forehead prints on my new 'Vette, please," he said. "I just had it detailed." He waited patiently as Hunter muttered something under his breath and exited the parked vehicle in a huff before lifting the power window back into position.

Winston Calhoun sat behind his vast onyx desk, elbows in front of him, fingers tented intently against his mouth. Kai, brown hair grown out to his neckline and limp, sat on a black leather couch near the door of Calhoun's office. When Hunter entered, the first thing he saw was Kai's face - tired, eyes and cheeks stained pink from previous blood-filled tears. Despite all his pent-up anger at Kai, seeing him in this state caused Hunter a twinge of pain.

"Agent Reeves," Calhoun said, "please have a seat." He motioned towards the sofa.

Hunter shifted his glance between Kai and Calhoun. "I'll stand, thanks," he said.

"Very well, but you may wish to change your mind in a few moments." Calhoun patted a manila file folder in front of his elbows on the desk. "As you know, we have been continuing on with the file digitization without your help. That includes the records of all other departments. Dr. Mugan has also been modernizing the medical records, and those include the DNA records. We've cross-referenced the DNA files of all the agents with any forensic evidence relevant to our past cases. *That* includes you."

Hunter's first instinct was a cruel one – take another jab at Kai, the easiest move. Make it hurt more. "Oh, is that so? What did we find – did Kai kill another relative I didn't know about?"

Kai gave a ragged sigh and put his face in his hands, but after a moment, he dropped them and looked directly at Hunter. His voice was soft, yet strained, and his words came faster than usual, as though he were trying to hold himself together through sheer momentum.

"Hunter," Kai began, his tone heavy with earnestness, "I know you're angry. You have every right to be. If I could undo what happened that night, I would. If I could trade places with your father, I would do it without hesitation. I... I had no way of knowing who he was to you at that time. He was just... a man. A man caught in the wrong place at the wrong time, and I... I thought I was doing the right thing, the merciful thing. He was dying, Hunter. He was in so much pain."

Kai's voice broke on the last word, and he paused, visibly struggling to contain the storm of emotions inside him. His hands gripped the edge of the couch tightly, his knuckles whitening. "I... I didn't know you existed. If I had, I would have fought harder to find another way. I would have... anything but what I did. But I didn't know, and now I have to live with the fact that my actions robbed you of a chance to know him."

Hunter stared at Kai, his anger battling with the unexpected pang of compassion he felt for the man before him. Kai's shoulders shook slightly as he continued. "I know that nothing I say or do will ever be enough. But I swear to you, Hunter, I would give anything to change it."

Kai's voice dropped to a whisper, and his head fell into his hands again. "I... I am so sorry."

"Save the sorries," Hunter said bitterly.

"Hunter!' Calhoun's sharp enunciation of his name caused Hunter to jolt. "I will *not* accept that tone or that insubordinate attitude against your superiors."

Hunter stiffened. Effectively chastised, he pursed his lips. "No, sir," he said.

Calhoun's tone softened. "No, Agent, it's ... more complicated than that," Calhoun said. "You see, we've determined that" –

"No, sir, I'll do it." Kai's voice was soft, yet strained. He was having trouble speaking clearly. He cleared his throat as he rose from the couch to speak to Hunter directly. "The clothes that Duncan was wearing the night... the night he died... have been locked away in evidence all this time. Mugan's team ran what blood and other materials were still on them, and the medical team was able to create a DNA profile. They added it to the computer, then ran a comparison between it and your DNA."

A pregnant pause hung in the air before Kai said, "There... there wasn't a match."

Hunter opened his mouth to speak, but he only felt a strange heat from his larynx, as if the muscles were grinding together, much like his teeth as he clasped his mouth shut again. When he finally located the words, he rasped, "What are you saying? I know that was him, I recognized the name in the file about the case at the mall - Duncan Reeves."

"I-I understand," Kai whispered softly. "But the forensics don't lie. Duncan Reeves was *not* your biological father like you had been led to believe."

Hunter's head began to feel heavy as he looked at Kai in his eyes. They were bright blue, conveying deep sorrow. All Hunter wanted at that moment was hold him, hug him tight to his chest and say he still loved him – but he still had all this anger inside.

"There's more, Hun," Kai gulped. "We also had your mother's file, you know, as part of the initial dossier we built when you became involved with The Order? Medical obtained her vital records from the county and added the data. They ran a comparison."

The heat was now churning in Hunter's gut. "W..what?"

"There was no match there, either, Hunter. Neither of them were your biological parents."

Hunter's face twisted, his brain abuzz with a flood of thoughts and potential actions. Simultaneously, he wanted to scream, to punch Kai in the face, to throw a chair through Calhoun's glass office walls. And through it all, a heat, an intense heat that would not ease up.

The room tilted, his vision swam, and the blood roared in his ears. Hunter's knees buckled, and he hit the ground with a heavy thud. Darkness claimed him, hot and all-consuming, dragging him into the depths of his unconscious mind.

Hunter opened his eyes to a curious and confusing sight.

He was... underwater? It felt like he was cold and wet. His surroundings were dark, but deeply blue. Was he in the ocean?

He kicked his legs to get his bearings, and found that he was freely able to swim. Kicking his legs again, he began to swim upward. Slowly but surely, he began to see more light as he approached what he assumed was the ocean surface.

Sunlight? Hunter hesitated; it would be bad news for him if it were sunlight. But, as he found himself getting colder and colder, he became perplexed - if he was nearing the sunlight, surely the water would be warming up, at least a degree or two?

Hunter thought he saw something dark and sloping ahead of him - a land mass, perhaps, or maybe a glacier or an iceberg. He'd try to swim toward that and climb above the surface. Thank heavens he didn't have to worry about the lack of oxygen!

It felt like miles upon miles, but as he approached the slope, he saw a thick sheet of ice, still transparent enough to let some light through. It was connected to the sloping mass, and as Hunter swam under it, he positioned himself so that he could stand against the slope and place his hands against the ice sheet.

He pressed. He pushed. It wouldn't budge. It wouldn't even crack. Looking at his hands, he willed the fingernails to grow into sharp claws, and began swiping furiously at the ice. Though the ice did shave underneath his claw tips, it was frustratingly little progress against the never-ending mattress of ice.

Get out of here, Hunter willed himself. *You have nothing but time – just claw your way out, no matter how long it takes.*

It felt like hours, maybe even days, but eventually Hunter managed to claw out a concave-shaped bowl from the block of ice. Hunter cracked his knuckles, preparing to try a series of punches to hopefully crack through to freedom.

But then a shadow appeared to block the strong, strange light emanating from above. Hunter strained his eyes to see what was the cause. It was ... a human? Or a humanoid shape? Hunter pushed a leg off the slope, inserting his head into the domed area to look closer.

The shadow shrunk as the object or being neared ever more. It looked familiar to Hunter, yet drastically different from the face he was now beginning to recognize.

"Kai?"

As if hearing the name, the figure raised his arms over his head. He was carrying a pickaxe with razor-sharp points.

Hunter started to shout out. The words, whatever they were, came out as a hopelessly muffled air bubble.

And then the figure swung, aiming for the thin part of the ice so helpfully carved out for him by his victim.

The pickaxe plunged easily through the ice, and split Hunter's skull in two. Hunter could feel the bone separating, bisecting his brain; he could feel the steel blade thrust into his brain stem.

Unable to do anything but float there, speared upon the pickaxe, Hunter watched as the water around him began to darken with his blood.

His body twitching involuntarily, he saw the man he recognized as Kai smile with a degree of sick satisfaction, then calmly walk away, leaving Hunter to squirm and twitch like a dying mouse caught under the metal snap of a trap.

The lights from above began to dim, bit by bit, until it was pitch black above.

As above, so below. Hunter bled out under the rapidly-refreezing water, pinned helplessly by the blade of the pickaxe.

When Hunter opened his eyes next, he found himself in a hospital gown in the familiar clinical setting of Dr. Mugan's office in the underground complex of The Order. Hunter last remembered being in Calhoun's office, which was, he calculated, seven floors and about three-quarters of a mile in steps away.

And he clearly hadn't walked there.

"What's going on?" As he said the words, it felt like fire was flying from his throat.

"You passed out," Dr. Mugan said, reaching in his pocket and producing a laser thermometer. "Hold still a second."

"Where's...?"

"I'm right here, young one," said Gibson, from a distance. Assuming Hunter's vantage point wasn't letting him see, Mugan stepped to his right. Gibson was seated in a folding chair against the far wall.

"What about...?"

"I'm here too, Hun." Mugan took another step, allowing Hunter to see Kai, who appeared even worse than he had been before Hunter lost consciousness.

Mugan clicked a button on his thermometer and read the results. He whistled. "One-eighteen," he said.

"What?!" The shout from Hunter's two boyfriends was immediate and sharp.

"I assume that's bad," Hunter said groggily.

Mugan shrugged. "It's about double the normal body temperature from a vampire at this hour of the evening." He pointed the device at the middle of his own forehead and clicked the trigger. He then showed the readout to Hunter.

"Sixty-nine," Hunter read out. "Nice."

Gibson put a comforting hand on Kai's shoulder. "He's making uncouth jokes," he said. "That has to be a good sign."

"It is," Mugan said, "inasmuch as he's lucid for now. Say what you've gotta say to him, chums – we're gonna have to move fast." He stepped out of the way to allow Kai and Gibson to take either side of Hunter's gurney.

"I'm getting rather tired of visiting the medical wing like this," Hunter rasped. He grimaced as he spoke; it felt like had a severe case of heartburn.

"Try not to speak," Gibson said. "It won't be pleasant until we can get you to a colder climate."

"Colder climate?" Kai seemed to be just as in the dark as Hunter about that statement. "What is going on here, Gibson?"

"He's breaking out," Gibson replied. He stroked his long black ponytail, which Hunter recognized as a sign that he was seriously concerned. "His inner demon is breaking out, I should say."

"Huh?" Hunter mumbled, trying to sit upright in bed.

"What does that mean?" Kai began to leak blood-red tears again.

"Age 30, 35 or so is about when a demon or cambion begins pubescence," Gibson explained. "Mine was... particularly rough; I may have wiped out a civilization or two."

"Let's continue this chat on the way to the helipad, gents," Mugan said, pulling up on the gurney's guardrails.

Hunter stared up at the ceiling as its tiles rushed past him, the heads of Mugan, Kai, and Gibson continuing to speak as they rushed out of the medical ward.

"It's the elemental part of a demon's overall personality," Gibson said. "The demon is best left in a secluded location to work it out with himself. One time, a fire demon I knew began breaking out and *should* have gone up to the Great Lakes to blaze out, but... let's just say he still owes the O'Leary descendants of Chicago a *lot* of remunerations."

"Am I gonna... blow up?" Hunter asked as they reached an elevator at the end of the hall.

The doors slid open to reveal a sleek, spacious interior, and Mugan pushed the gurney inside. Unlike standard elevators, this one had no visible buttons for individual floors, just a complex touch interface with a glowing map. As the elevator began its ascent, it shifted smoothly to the side, moving not just upward but also diagonally through the complex. Hunter's head lolled back against the gurney as he stared at the faintly illuminated panels lining the walls.

"I keep forgetting the elevators here aren't normal," Hunter murmured, the faint wisp of smoke escaping his lips again.

"No, you won't blow up, sweetie," Gibson said, looking down and giving Hunter a reassuring smile. Gibson then looked across at the other side of the gurney and to Kai, who was staring at the swirls of smoke dissipating around them. "I swear, he's not. Though he's gonna be as conspicuous and flashy as a Fourth of July fireworks show." He gestured to the tendrils of smoke coming out of Hunter's nostrils to illustrate his point.

"Which is why we're going to fly him out to our base at Matthew Island," Mugan said, punching a series of buttons on the elevator control panel. "It's uninhabited and it's below freezing all day 'round this time of year."

"*Alaska?*" Hunter recognized the name of the area from his dual-credit geography class in high school. "So what, you're flying me out and dumping me in the middle of nowhere, Alaska?"

"It's for the best, really, based on what Gibson's briefed me about," Mugan said, guiding the troop out of the elevator as it dinged to a halt. The blustery air of the helipad greeted them all. It actually felt comfortable to Hunter, after all the recent flare-ups of heat. "And you won't technically be alone."

The elevator doors opened. As Mugan steered the gurney toward the helicopter waiting several hundred yards away, he added, "You know, they don't cover this in med school. 'What to do when your patient starts combusting' wasn't exactly a chapter in the textbook."

A red pulse of light groaned to life from under Hunter's hospital gown, around the area where his new tattoo sat. All four of them stared at the light.

"What the...?" Hunter whispered.

"Ya'll are gonna be paying me *triple* for this," shouted a gruff voice. "Possibly quadruple. Likely quadruple."

Hunter lifted his head as much as he was able.

Slicer stood cavalierly out of the seat of the waiting helicopter, beckoning with the palm of his hand.

"Let's get the patient loaded up."

Mugan advised Kai on how to adjust the gurney's legs so they would fold up as they lifted and slid it–and Hunter– into the helicopter. He then politely yet firmly shouted orders to Slicer over the whir of the rotors, and Slicer buckled Hunter securely to the gurney, and locked the wheels of the gurney into place.

The doctor stepped toward Kai and Gibson, pulling them in for a close huddle. As they broke apart, Mugan jogged toward the pilot seat of the helicopter.

"Do you want to go first?" Gibson asked Kai.

Kai, still looking much worse for wear, shook his head. "I'm sure he doesn't want to see me," he said. "You can go."

Gibson nodded, then walked towards the chopper's cabin. Kai watched as he climbed aboard the cabin. The noise of the helicopter and the blustering wind made it impossible to hear from his vantage point, but he did see as Hunter and Gibson traded sentences. He watched as Gibson took both of Hunter's hands and squeezed them, but as Gibson leaned forward to kiss Hunter's lips, he turned to one side. *That* was too much. He fixated on a piece of brightly yellow-painted asphalt at the edge of the helipad.

Moments passed, and Gibson returned, tapping Kai on the shoulder.

"Are they about to take off, then?" Kai could barely speak the words.

"Not yet," Gibson said, with the slightest of smiles. "He wants to speak with you."

Kai's undead heart lurched upward. "He does?"

Gibson nodded and gingerly wrapped a hand around to Kai's back, pushing him toward the chopper. "Hurry."

Kai raced to the cabin at vampire speed, which caused Slicer, sitting behind Hunter's head, to flinch. "Damn. I hate when you guys do that," he muttered.

Hunter looked at Kai, gazing upon the state his face and body were in. His lower lip quivered, and for a moment, he seemed unable to find the words. Finally, he spoke, his voice hoarse and trembling. "I'm scared," he admitted, his glowing green eyes denoting sincerity and honesty meeting Kai's.

Kai bit his lip, his mind racing for the right thing to say, the right way to comfort Hunter. "I know," he said softly, stepping closer and resting a hand on Hunter's arm. "I know you are."

"I... I don't know how to handle this," Hunter continued, his voice breaking. "It's like I'm not even myself anymore. I feel like I'm just... burning up inside, and it's hurting everyone around me." He paused, his glowing irises flickering like embers. "I didn't mean to hurt you, Kai. I'm so sorry."

Kai's chest tightened, and for a moment, he couldn't speak. The raw vulnerability in Hunter's voice was almost too much to bear. Finally, he leaned down, cupping Hunter's face with both hands. "You don't have to apologize," he said firmly. "I know what this is. I know what you're going through, and none of it changes how I feel about you."

Tears welled in Hunter's eyes, slipping down his cheeks. "But I've been so... so selfish. So angry—"

"Shhh," Kai interrupted, pressing a finger gently to Hunter's lips. "It's okay. You don't have to explain. I've been where you are, Hunter. I know what it's like to feel like you're coming apart at the seams." He took a deep, shuddering breath, his own blood-red tears mixing with the glow of the helicopter's interior lights. "And I'm here. I'm not going anywhere."

Hunter let out a shaky breath, his hand reaching up to cover Kai's. "I still love you," he whispered. "I need you to know that."

Kai smiled through his tears, leaning down to press his forehead against Hunter's. "I love you too," he said, his voice barely above a whisper. "And I always will."

They stayed like that for a moment, foreheads touching, hands clasped, as the world around them blurred into the roar of the helicopter's rotors. Finally, Kai pulled back, his smile soft but resolute. "You focus on getting better, okay? We'll get through this together."

Hunter nodded, his lips curving into a faint, grateful smile. "I'll try."

Kai kissed him, slow and tender, pouring every ounce of his love and reassurance into the gesture. When he pulled back, he wiped away his tears and stood, his resolve hardening. "You're going to be okay," he said firmly, giving Hunter one last squeeze of his hand before stepping back out of the cabin.

As the door slid shut, Kai turned to Slicer, his face set with determination. "Take care of him," he said.

Slicer gave a curt nod. "You got it." Patting Hunter on a very, very warm ankle, Slicer added, "Just keep breathing, kid. We'll get you there in one piece–preferably just glowing, not burning."

Trotting back to Gibson at the far edge of the helipad, Kai watched the helicopter lift off and begin its journey to the airport.

"I can't believe how warm he felt," Kai said, running a hand through his hair. He began to walk toward the access door leading back into the building.

"I know. It was very worrisome." Gibson reached into his pants pocket as he followed Kai and produced a cloth handkerchief. "Here, for the…" he gestured at his eyes and handed the cloth to Kai.

"Thanks." Kai dabbed at his eyes. "Uh, listen. I don't… um. I don't want to go back to my place tonight. At least, not right away."

Gibson's eyebrows arched. "What's up?"

Kai took a belabored sigh and opened the access door as they reached it. "Our cat passed away last night."

The surprised look on Gibson's face changed quickly to one of concern. "Oh, no. Belle, was it?"

"Annabelle," Kai corrected. "But yes."

They began to descend the staircase.

"That's rough," Gibson said. "I'm not quite the cat person myself, but I know you and Hunter are – does he know?"

Kai shook his head. "I figure this should wait. Something like this could disturb his emotional state, such as it is."

"Quite right," Gibson said. As they came to the landing and continued on toward the elevator, he pressed the call button. After a short silence, he added, "You could always come over to the condo," he offered. "If you need a brief change of scenery. If you want to talk."

The elevator chimed and the doors opened. They walked in and the doors closed.

After a few awkward moments of silence, Gibson finally asked, "What's in your files?"

Kai cocked his head, caught off-guard. "Pardon?"

"You said that Hunter's read your file," Gibson said. "What happened in your first decades?"

"It's not really any of your business." The edge in Kai's voice surprised him. So, too, was the pang of guilt he felt when he saw Gibson's expression. Ever since Gibson had defected from The Crown, Kai had conducted himself with a certain amount of disdain toward the new agent. This was, after all, the vampire responsible, albeit indirectly, for influencing some of The Crown's most dangerous and violent operatives to do what they did.

But Kai had since learned Gibson's reasons to leave The Crown were genuine. And he *had* taken Hunter under his wing when the powers on Hunter's demonic side began to emerge.

Kai reckoned Gibson was genuinely reaching out.

"Before I was known as Kai, my given name was Caeden," he said. "I was turned against my will around the time of the Civil War. Then my maker, my sire, was killed. I spent the first three decades and change running wild."

"You're kidding," Gibson said with a degree of amazement. "I've known many a vamp who went mad in the first three years living as a rogue, much less three *decades*. What led you out of that mind trap – and how'd you wind up with The Order?"

Kai rubbed his sunken, exhausted eyes and sighed. "It's a tremendously long story."

"I've got the time," Gibson offered as the elevator dinged and the doors opened, emptying them out into the parking garage.

3
THE FLEDGLING

Autumn 1900 - Near Pigeon Forge, Tennessee
Caeden Taylor had already been used to this scenario before: seated around a campfire, flanked by a group of vampires, telling his story. He warned them, as he had at least a half dozen times to half a dozen other tribes over the past 38 years, that he had trouble controlling himself. He wasn't a good person.

"You're not a *person* anymore," said the Latino woman directly across from him. "You must remember that. You are Vampire."

"He's rogue, Olivia, is what he is," growled the grizzled, wrinkly-faced man to her right. He eyed Caeden with a degree of revulsion that Caeden instantly knew was deserved.

"It's not his fault, William," Olivia snapped. "His *sire* was the rogue." She turned to face Caeden with a kindly smile. "Has anyone ever told you exactly what the rogue is?"

Caeden held his hands up to the campfire and shook his head no. He gazed to his left to find a younger man -

much younger in appearance than William, and taller - who smiled at him sweetly.

"We see rogues as the... scourge of our kind. Predators in every sense of the word, preying upon the helpless. He saw you in the water and felt you were the weakest, the easiest to turn into his kind.

"Had he survived to teach you his ways," Olivia continued, "you would have learned how to feed indiscriminately, without any sense of decorum or subtlety. You would have acted out of a desire to do harm, to be evil."

"Haven't you heard a word the kid's told us?" William growled again. "Feeding at will's all he's done for 40 years!"

"That's not the same thing, William," Olivia sighed patiently as Caeden's head swam. He was trying to process what he was told: After years of the killing he was already responsible for – he'd lost count of how many creatures over the years... farm animals, mostly, but certainly some humans too – *that* wasn't necessarily evil? He would have been *taught* what was truly evil, and would have been doing *that* instead?

"It's okay," Olivia said comfortingly. She looked to Caeden like a grandmother-type, her black hair tied into a tight bun, a few metal earrings dangling from her lobes, making cheerful jangles as she moved her head. "I understand it's been rough. It won't be a fast process. But, if you stay with my nest, we can improve your chances for continued survival. Isn't that right, Spencer?"

"Of course," said the younger looking boy, who up to this point hadn't taken his eyes of Caeden. Ignoring

William's disapproving look, Spencer stood up and reached out a hand, patting it against Caeden's shoulder. Caeden could see dark freckles against Spencer's lightly brown-skinned cheeks.

The four spent the next few hours getting better acquainted. Olivia had been a vampire for the better part of the last century. Olivia and her maker had traveled north from Mexico in the hopes of reaching Canada and its longer, darker winters.

The other two were brothers - Spencer was the older of the two, despite looking like William's son. But Spencer had been a vampire much longer, and had come back to claim his brother after learning of the rest of his family's death. They happened to cross paths with Olivia, whose maker had just recently been killed.

"It was in battle with a rogue," Olivia said. "A vampire is quite strong, but a rogue cannot control his strength. It was like a powder keg exploded. My maker could not get out of the way in time, and he lost his head in the rogue's fury."

"My god," Caeden breathed.

"Since then," William said, not so much *at* Caeden but in his general vicinity, "we have roamed the lands as we make our way to the northern border. We explore when we can, feeding only on who we must."

"We had stayed in the Deep South for quite some time," Spencer chimed in, smiling softly at Caeden. "But with my having lived off the wounded during the War Between the States, I had become to accustomed to it. I was proving to be a bad example to my brother after I turned him. We found ourselves preying on anyone who was even the slightest bit injured."

Olivia nodded and leaned towards Caeden, pulling a knitted shawl around his shoulders. "Even for our kind, seeing the effects of war can be toxic to our nature and can cause us to slip into rogue tendencies."

"But when you're already there..." William sneered.

"William. Enough." Olivia's tone sharpened. Where she had been motherly and tender just seconds ago, Caeden could tell her patience was breaking. "I think he understands why we're against rogues. And I think that's enough chat for now. Sun's close to rising. We should go to ground, yes?"

As the four of them rose, Caeden followed Olivia downstream to gather water to douse the campfire.

"I saw my maker staked," he offered. "Even though I don't even know his name, I don't think I can ever forget the sight of it. Anytime I close my eyes, I can see the blackness. I see the blackness of his remains..."

Olivia nodded matronly as she dipped a small bucket into the river water. "It is brutal, to be sure. However, I hope you don't take offense when I say that your maker truly had it coming."

"No offense taken at all," Caeden said. Though he had come to terms with the fact he was a vampire, and nothing could ever reverse it, he would always remain bitter to some degree that he never had a choice in the matter.

Making their way back to camp, Olivia said in a low voice, "I would like to extend to you an invitation to stay with my nest and travel with us toward Canada."

Caeden went rigid. He'd been in this position before. And it never ended well. "Are you sure? I mean, I would hate to intrude..."

"Given your history and your circumstances, I would insist upon it," she replied. "When a vampire sires, he or she must put some, if not most of their blood inside their new charge. That blood becomes your blood – for better or for worse – and it carries with it the traits of the maker. Rogue blood will forever run through your veins. It became *you*. You run a constant risk of breaking out as a full rogue due to how potent the blood is. But with guidance, there is a better chance you can survive it. All it takes is a tutor."

Caeden smiled softly. "I wouldn't want to wind up a monster," he said with a small and awkward laugh. "I will take any help you are willing to provide."

"Splendid. You're already on the right path."

Back at camp, Caeden took the water bucket from Olivia and doused the flames, sending a plume of white smoke skyward. He took a nearby stick and stirred the water and ash into a sludge. As he stirred, he let his mind wander, only to be snapped back to attention when he felt a tap on his shoulder.

"May I?" Spencer held out his hand, motioning for the bucket. Caeden passed it to him, and Spencer knelt to the ground, scooping a few handfuls of sand and dirt into the tin receptacle. He then emptied the bucket over the few embers still glowing in the fire pit.

"Is William already in the ground?" Olivia asked.

"Mmhmm," Spencer murmured. Glancing at Caeden, he added, "He behaves like a brute, I know. I suppose I should apologize for the way he's spoken and behaved toward you."

Overhearing, Olivia stepped nearer. "He will come around, in time," she said. "Speaking of ground, that is where I am heading. Don't dawdle much longer, you two. I shall see you tomorrow evening."

The two young-looking men bid their goodbyes to Olivia, and then sat the fire pit a bit longer, watching the few weak wisps of smoke that remained escape the smothered kindling.

"I don't suppose there's a bed waiting for me back there," Caeden said, waving a hand towards the clearing where Olivia was already preparing to step into a hand-dug trench, pulling clumps of dirt upon herself. Burying herself.

"Not yet, you don't," Spencer replied. "But I don't mind helping you dig one out."

"I appreciate it."

"That way, you can be sure to sleep next to me." The comment was so innocent, so off-handed, that Caeden barely registered the meaning underneath it. Only when Caeden looked at Spencer and saw the blush and the coy grin on his face did Caeden felt a strange fluttering sensation across his stomach, as if he would *like* the idea of sleeping beside Spencer... and not just in the context of a dirt plot next to one another.

An urge to pursue the curious nature of the thought planted itself in Caeden's head, but he decided he was too tired to explore it. Instead, he allowed Spencer to lead a path toward their "beds" – simple grave-sized plots of earth underneath some tall trees. They knelt to an undisturbed patch of land next to the last open pit, and began to dig at the earth. Caeden tested the hole a few times, and once it felt comfortable enough for him to lay in, Spencer helped cover himself in the dirt. Moments later, he was sound asleep.

For the first six months of his time with them, Caeden followed behind the other three travelers, almost like a caboose, as they traversed the hinterland against the flow of the river, crossing two states as they did so. Every other night, Olivia or William would test Caeden's strength and teach him how to best his occasional urges to act out, avoiding the risk of giving in to the rogue instincts deep within himself.

Feedings became rarer as the group got further into the plains. An occasional deer could be found here and there, and once in a blue moon, they might encounter a buffalo whose blood would satiate them for a good while. The lack of steady food taught Caeden the importance of maintaining his energy level. As Olivia said to him, "the fewer resources you have now, the better. A rogue would gorge himself and lose all that precious energy very quickly."

William's attitude toward Caeden also improved, once he saw that the new vampire was indeed trying and making progress. William found Caeden a well-behaved and attentive student, taking correction as advice intended to prolong his life – not as nitpicking. Despite this, William would still not readily engage Caeden in discussion or chatter. He left that to Spencer, although William had unspoken concerns about that relationship.

Those worries were not totally unfounded, as even Olivia could readily see something developing between 'her two boys,' as she sometimes referred to them. Spencer found himself wanting to be around Caeden more than he did his brother. Beyond the new guy being a bit calmer and convivial than William, Spencer also found Caeden's naturally inquisitive nature refreshing. Caeden was always wondering why some vampires did things a certain way, and other groups behaved differently.

When Olivia and William and Spencer shared stories about their experiences feeding off other humans, Caeden could be relied upon to ask about how the humans were treated: Were they scared? Were they left in pain afterward? Did they have families? While William often found this line of questioning a pesterance, Spencer admired Caeden's desire to know more.

Spencer began to wonder what it might feel like to be alone with Caeden more often. Perhaps he could sit closer to him one night, maybe even rest his head upon Caeden's arm? As innocent as those scenarios seemed, there was an annoying part of Spencer's brain that said he shouldn't act upon those daydreams. What if Caeden didn't reciprocate? What if they made him angry – maybe even enough to trigger a rage and push him over the edge, finally making him a full-on rogue?

One hot summer night, after a particularly grueling and unproductive hunt, Olivia announced she was retiring to ground earlier than usual. William, as had become habit since Caeden's first night with them, had been the first to begin his slumber.

"Are you two coming with?" Olivia inquired.

"Actually, if you don't mind," Spencer began, "I thought it might be nice to go for a swim in the river? To try and relax in the cool water."

"That's fine," came the reply. "Just be on guard for any threats while you're on your own. Snakebites can disorient vampires like you wouldn't believe!"

"Oh, Caeden," Spencer grabbed him by the arm as he passed by. "Would you... maybe... would you mind joining me?"

Startled by the question, Caeden stammered for a few moments. "Uh, sure, I guess. That'd be fine," he managed to spit out.

"That's a fine idea," Olivia said, tightening her hair bun. "Strength in numbers. Just remember" –

"Be in ground before sunrise," Spencer, Olivia, and Caeden said in unison before sharing a hearty laugh. This had become routine between the three for some time now. Caeden found it genuinely funny, and a little bit endearing. It reminded him, for the first time since his human life ended, of a memory from that time period: His mother would ask him every morning to hurry up and start his chores at the farmhouse. "Yes, mother," he would always say from underneath a mound of covers. "I'll be down in another few moments."

Her reply would always be, "Mind that you do. Remember: A moment astray is a moment without play."

Spencer hugged Olivia goodnight. Then, after he saw she had gone below ground, he whispered to Caeden, "Thanks for agreeing to come with me. I was almost afraid you'd say no."

"Why would I say no?" Caeden laughed. "It's probably as hot now as it was a few hours ago. I could use a good cooling off."

"Then let's see who cools off first!" Spencer grinned and took off at top vampiric speed, leaving a shirt to flutter in the still air and hit the ground at Caeden's feet. Delaying himself only to watch the shirtless blur land with a gleeful yelp in the water, Caeden took a flying leap, heading straight for the water without setting foot back on solid ground.

The splash was so immense it caught Caeden off guard, and he somersaulted upon contacting the water. His rear end bounced off the river floor underneath him. His head broke above the surface a moment later and he let out a hearty laugh. Spencer joined in the laughter too, and a few minutes were spent in playful, childlike tackling, with splashes percussing the air as they flailed about.

When the initial excitement abated, and they were just two men standing in a river, they began to tread water and talk. Caeden went into more detail about how he left home at the start of the Civil War, lying about his age in order to gain entry into the navy, and his time aboard the Monitor before its destruction.

"Did you ever kill anyone while you were at war?" Spencer asked.

"Not personally," Caeden said. "The most I ever did on that ship was swab the deck. Well," he said, correcting himself. "Until the final battle we undertook. It was a few days before the sinking. I was called upon to load artillery into place. I even fired off a round myself, but it didn't hit anything, I don't think."

Spencer nodded as he listened to Caeden's words, kicking his heels up through the water and starting to float. He gazed up at the heavens and the few stars that were starting to peek out from an otherwise cloudy summer night. "I have killed a few in my time," he said.

Caeden wasn't sure by his tone whether that was a boast or a confession. "I'm sure it's an eventuality," he said. "I hadn't thought about it much, but if this is what I am – a vampire – I'd expect killing to be unavoidable."

"That doesn't mean I would ever enjoy it," Spencer replied, looking earnestly at Caeden. His words were soaked with emotion. Without further warning, Spencer's eyes began to glow. The brown coloring of his eyes changed in a flash to a stellar shade of emerald green, complete with light.

It was a sight Caeden had not seen in all this time as a loner. He stared at Spencer's face, transfixed. "How did you do that?"

Spencer seemed confused, but then his face finally registered understanding. "My eyes changed color," he said, looking into the rippling river water to see his reflection. "It's a visceral reaction we vampires have. We can't help it; and I don't know one yet who can control it. Every color is tied to an emotion. If we generate light, it is particularly strong. At least, that's how Olivia explains it. Green means fear and/or sorrow. Guess which one for me?" He chuckled softly, then began to frown.

"Hey, hey." Caeden paddled a bit closer toward Spencer. "I know I'm the new one here, but I knew when I enlisted there would be the chance I'd be responsible for someone's death. It's quite the same situation here."

"It's going to be so much more difficult for you now, though," Spencer said, biting his lower lip. "The way Olivia says it, each time you have contact with a human from here on out, and especially when you intend to feed on them, you risk rogue power overtaking you completely!"

"Even if that's true," Caeden responded, "the three of you are doing such a great job telling me how to fight it, and how to persevere. With that kind of support, I know I can behave." He smiled, gazing back toward Spencer.

By now, Spencer's eyes had reverted back to their original deep brown. They were slipping below Caeden's face and onto the water in between them.

"You're... you're holding my hand," Spencer said, softly. As if to prove his point, Spencer lifted his arm above the water. As he said, Caeden's hand was tightly wrapped around Spencer's.

"Oh – I'm sorry," Caeden blushed, almost in disbelief. "I didn't realize." He tried to unthread his fingers from Spencer's.

Spencer responded by tightening the grip. "Don't be sorry," he breathed. "I... I like how it feels."

Caeden gulped. He searched his mind for something to say. "I'm ... I'm kind of sorry that the green light faded from your eyes," he eventually said. "It looked about as nice as your brown eyes do."

He instantly regretted his words; if he had a functioning circulatory system, this would be the point at which he would be blushing. Another tangled rush of thoughts flew through his mind. What was he feeling? Was it simple care, triggered from the sensation of a hand being held? Was he feeling these things as an adoptive brother? A close friend, perhaps? Maybe something deeper, perhaps romantic? Maybe he feels the same.

No, don't start thinking this way, he chided himself. You'll complicate matters even further. He decided he would not push himself to ask questions of Spencer. There would be little point in trying to compare notes. *When I held your hand, what did* you *think that meant?*

Spencer hesitated, his gaze fixed on the dying campfire. "Caeden," he murmured, his voice trembling just enough to catch Caeden's attention.

"Yeah?" Caeden shifted closer, his unease melting into concern.

"Can I–" Spencer faltered, his cheeks tinged pink. "Could I... just for a moment?" He gestured vaguely, his vulnerability clear.

Caeden's chest tightened. He didn't trust himself–not with Spencer, not with anyone. But the quiet plea in Spencer's eyes was impossible to ignore.

Wordlessly, Caeden opened his arms. Spencer stepped into them cautiously, his head resting against Caeden's shoulder.

"You're warmer than I expected," Spencer whispered, his breath tickling Caeden's neck.

Caeden let out a soft, self-deprecating laugh. "Don't get used to it."

As they stood there, the weight of the moment pressed down on Caeden. He felt the pull of something dangerous yet undeniable—a fleeting connection that he couldn't afford to indulge.

The pair enjoyed each other's company, as well as the modest intimacy, until the faintest of pink rays began to lift over the horizon.

"I wish this night would never end," Caeden said as they broke their embrace.

Spencer smiled, his eyes dipping bashfully. "That's exactly what I was about to say."

They swam to the riverbank and climbed out of the water. After some brisk, vampire-speed shaking to advance the drying-off process, Caeden and Spencer rushed to their underground beds before the dawning rays of the morning sun reached their bodies.

They held hands the whole way there. It only took a few seconds to reach the dirt pits, but Caeden enjoyed every fleeting moment – and he knew in his undead heart that Spencer did as well.

As the group settled in to shield themselves from the impending day, Caeden spent a few more moments above ground, staring at the stars, his thoughts tangled. Spencer's warmth still lingered in his arms, a sensation both comforting and terrifying.

A rustle in the woods snapped his attention away. His instincts sharpened, his eyes scanning the shadows.

Nothing.

And yet, the unease didn't fade. A whisper at the back of his mind—rogue blood, perhaps, or impending danger? He couldn't be sure. But a nagging thought stayed with him as he buried himself under the dirt: this fragile peace probably wouldn't last long.

4
OCCLUDED FRONT

Hunter knew he was in a dream state again, but also knew he had been sedated and couldn't force himself out of it this time.

This isn't real, he repeated to himself. *This isn't going to hurt.*

He seemed to be suspended in mid-air, laying with his back to the ground... if there was one. It was so dark, he could barely make out any details, but he could feel from the force of gravity that he was facing upward.

He could also feel the binds of something - wire, rope, chain? - keeping him in place. He could feel hundreds of razor-sharp metallic teeth digging into his flesh from almost every place he could feel sensation. Despite what he told himself moments ago, he could feel pain. The metal seared with the slightest of movements.

Silver.

Gritting his teeth, Hunter willed himself to stay as still as possible. Just when he thought he was getting the hang of doing so, pure sunlight filled the chamber, stinging his eyes and causing him to react naturally, trying to lift his arms to his face.

The pained screams of two other male voices caused him to put his arms back immediately. He strained to get his eyes accustomed to the light to see who was in the room with him. In doing so, he could immediately feel that something was keeping his eyes pulled open. But he also knew from the tone of the voices exactly who was there: Kai and Gibson. They sounded distant... and in distress.

He was staring up at a labyrinthian web of silver rope, each strand pulled to its fullest extent. There was absolutely no slack between any strand. And every single rope was connected to his body, his naked body, by alligator clamps that looked as if they had been welded to his skin.

Hunter followed the path of one rope from his eyeline - he thought this one was clamped onto one of his pectoral muscles - and traced it through the maze. It seemed to end somewhere near Gibson's face.

"Don't... move... any... further." Gibson's voice was muffled, as if he were speaking through clenched teeth.

"What the" – was all Hunter could manage before an electrical charge flushed through his body, making him shout in panic. His left arm jerked involuntarily. Almost the exact same moment, he could hear Kai scream –shriek, even–in agony.

Hunter tried to ask the other two what was going on via their shared telepathy, but it wasn't working.

"Ropes... electrified. Disrupting... telepathy." Kai's voice was ragged, pained. "Don't... move," he echoed.

Gibson yelled out next, and Hunter immediately felt the metallic teeth of an alligator clamp pulling up on his right eyelid. "Aaaaargh," he grimaced. It felt like the skin was tearing from his head. After a second or two, which felt like an eternity, the eyelid and its connected wire settled back to normal.

"We're... connected." Gibson said, jaw set tight. "Can't move... without... hurting... each other."

As if some outside force was demonstrating his point, Gibson screamed out as an electrical pulse was fed into his body. He tried to fight the physical reaction, but it was no use - his neck twitched, and the metallic rope connected to his neck jerked along with it. This rope split into two different directions: one in Kai's direction, the other in Hunter's.

Hunter felt the skin on his own neck peel away as the metal rope connected to it was pulled. He hollered in agony. Hearing Kai scream at exactly the same time, he assumed, rightly, an identical fate befell Kai.

"How do we... stop this?" Hunter groaned between clenched teeth.

"Finish what you started," echoed an unfamiliar voice. The words reverberated around the chamber, seeming to land on Hunter's ears specifically.

"What?"

"Do what you went to the club that night to do," the voice purred into Hunter's ear. It was a comforting sounding voice, coaxing and soft. But the words dripped with vile meaning to Hunter.

The sound of a crank being turned replaced the unfamiliar voice, and Hunter felt himself being lifted into a sitting position. There were ropes attached to his back, and he could feel the clamps dig into his shoulders and lower spinal column. There were more screams from above, as Kai and Gibson were torturously contorted in kind.

The crank stopped, and Hunter's arms, hands in a clasped position on his lap, came into his view. They were not bound by anything. A pulsating noise began to creep behind Hunter, and before he could stop himself, he twisted his body to look in the direction of the noise.

The silver cables were gone. So were Gibson and Kai.

Hunter was looking at a door. A bathroom door.

The pulsating noise he was hearing was a club mix of one of his favorite songs, muzzled and diminished by the door.

Hunter looked down at his body. He was fully clothed. He remembered the outfit well. It was a pair of his comfy denim jeans and his favorite Coheed & Cambria live tour shirt.

He was back in Electric Six, the downtown Dallas gay club he had frequented as a human; it was also where he first met Kai.

Hunter was sitting on the floor of the club's bathroom, just like he had been at one point on the night he met Kai. The night everything changed.

"You're human again," said the voice. "Just in this moment. Time enough to do the deed."

Tears began to flow from Hunter's face. Clear tears. Salty tears. Human tears. Tears that caused his vision to blur. He looked down at his lap, his hands, his fingers, and a small piece of metal quivered into an unrecognizable melange of dull colors.

"Do it," the voice intoned, sounding more sinister than the last time Hunter heard it. "Finish what you started."

Hunter's heartbeat pounded in time with the beat of the song playing outside. He looked down at his arms, draped loosely over his legs. His left arm was palm up, wrist and forearm skin pale, the artery leading from his hand pulsating with life. Human life.

His right hand was clenched tight, the thumb and forefinger clutching the piece of metal, which glinted in the lamplight of the restroom.

A razor blade.

"Tell me," said the voice. "Why on earth would you do it in the club toilets?"

His tears flowing like rivers, Hunter tried to shake the question away. He continued to stare at his arms - the one hand gripping the blade, the other waiting patiently.

"I know why." The voice began to sound playful and coy. "The poetic license. This is where you proposed. This is where that Alex character broke up with you. The scene of your *ultimate* humiliation. The latest indignity." There was a cruel chuckle as the voice added, "as if bleeding out in a dirty bathroom would show them all."

"Shut up," Hunter growled. He threw the razor blade across the room. As it plinked and clattered to a stop, Hunter flew to the door and tried to open it - but there was no handle. He pushed, but it didn't budge. He gave it a vampiric kick - but his human foot only bristled in pain as it connected with the solid door. Frustrated, he trudged to the bathroom sink.

The blade was there, waiting, in the soap divot.

"You thought becoming a vampire would help," the voice chortled with glee. "You honestly thought becoming immortal would free you from the memory of *all your failures in life?* You're such an idiot."

"Stop it," Hunter pleaded. As he stared at himself in the mirror, his eyes began to change colors from violet to a pallid gray... then seeming to blink into a glowing amber, then an intense purple, then back to gray. The image in the mirror was glitching like a broken computer screen.

It began to sound as if the disembodied voice was more inside his head than out. "And you become *this?* A secret agent vampire man? A mere distraction. No matter what you do, you'll always be a half-wit. A half-breed. A half *demon!*"

"Stop it!"

Hunter shut his eyes tight and shook his head. Opening his eyes, he stared into the mirror, his reflection blurred by the bathroom's dim, flickering light. The edges of the glass seemed to ripple, and then it emerged –a dark, churning presence behind him. The shadow loomed, its form fluid yet menacing, eyes glowing crimson and a grin splitting its jagged face.

"You look tired, Hunter," it whispered, voice slick with mockery. "Did the weight of being... unwanted finally catch up to you?"

"Go away," Hunter muttered, his voice brittle.

The shadow's grin widened, its voice dropping to a conspiratorial purr. "But I'm part of you, remember? I only say what you're already thinking."

Hunter's jaw tightened as he tried to focus on the crack in the tile floor, anything but the searing words.

"Poor boy," the shadow continued, circling him. "You didn't even notice, did you? The way she looked at you—like something she had to endure. And now that she's gone, you're left with the truth. You weren't hers. You weren't anyone's. Just a mistake no one wanted to claim."

Hunter's chest tightened, the air around him suddenly heavy. "She loved me," he rasped.

The shadow's laugh reverberated through the room. "She pitied you. There's a difference. And even she couldn't fix what's broken inside you." It leaned closer, its form seeping into the edges of the mirror. "That's why you're here, isn't it? You're hoping someone, anyone, will care enough to make it stop."

Hunter turned from the mirror, hands clutching his head. "Shut up!"

"But it won't stop," the shadow hissed, sliding across the walls, its tendrils dark and relentless. "No one's coming to save you. No one cares enough to even try. Except me."

Hunter froze as the shadow's voice softened, almost tender. "I can help you, Hunter. I can make the pain stop. All it takes is one small step." A dark tendril nudged the blade on the sink forward, its metallic glint catching Hunter's eye.

His breath hitched, his hands trembling as he stared at it.

"Think about it," the shadow urged, its voice soothing now, coaxing. "No more loneliness. No more wondering where you came from or why you're like this. Just peace. Doesn't that sound nice?"

Hunter's fingers twitched, drawn to the blade's cold promise. His reflection in the mirror stared back at him, hollow-eyed and fractured.

"You know it's the only way," the shadow murmured, its presence pressing down like a vice. "Do it, and you'll finally be free."

For a moment, the room seemed to freeze, the blade almost calling to him. But something deep inside flickered–a fragile, defiant spark.

"No," Hunter said, his voice barely above a whisper. He reached out, grabbed the blade, and hurled it across the room again. It clattered against the wall and fell to the floor, far from reach.

The shadow's form wavered, its grin twisting into something almost disappointed. "Coward," it spat, retreating into the mirror's depths. "You can't escape me, Hunter. I'll always be here, waiting for the day you finally listen."

With a chilling laugh, it vanished, leaving Hunter alone in the dim bathroom.

Hunter sank to the floor, his knees pressing into the cold tile. His chest heaved, his hands trembling. He could hear voices from outside the nightclub, from the alleyway behind the restroom. He knew at once who one of the voices belonged to – it was Alex, his ex-boyfriend, the man he thought he ultimately would marry once upon a time. He was trying to sell information to someone; it was the mission Kai was there that night to monitor and the mission Hunter had interrupted.

His first instinct, as it was the night this first happened, was to go to the toilet, step on the seat and try to open the frosted ventilation window to peek outside.

A tremendous wind filled the small room, and before Hunter had a chance to react, he found himself in the grip of the shadow's form. The shadow had pulled Hunter back to the sink and pulled his head back by the hair, exposing his throat.

"Have you ever considered the throat instead of the wrists, by the way?" The shadow chortled as it traced a foggy tendril of a finger across Hunter's Adam's apple. Its voice regained a hint of softness, of sensuality. "Of course you have. I listened to your thoughts all through high school, all through college. So many times I thought you'd go for the gusto... and you'd wimp out at the last minute. Afraid of leaving a mess? Or just afraid you wouldn't do it right? Like all the other times. Well, why don't you just let me do it for you? I'm stronger than you now."

Staring into the mirror, Hunter watched as the shadowy figure picked up the blade, which once more found its way back to the sink, and drew it closer.

"You... are *not* stronger than me." Hunter growled.

The wind picked up again, and the grip on Hunter's body fell away. Hunter whirled around, his back to the sink. The shadowy form now stood at the bathroom door.

"Keep thinking that, vampire boy," it said. "Be wrong, again. As usual. When you finally tire of fighting it out,

I'll find you. Just remember this – not even the immortal want to deal with someone with as many issues as you. All you're gonna do is cause them pain."

The shadow dissipated into a fine mist, and the lights to the restroom were cut off, plunging Hunter into pitch darkness. Hunter could hear fresh screams from his two lovers echo and hurtle toward him in a deafening wave.

The sensation of Hunter's back hitting virgin snow, followed by a sizzling sound and the feeling of his body being consumed by ice water sent him snapping to attention. There was steam clouding his field of vision, but he could hear a pair of familiar voices:

"Mother of *fuck*!" Slicer exclaimed. "How hot has he gotten?"

Mugan's voice came next: "My sensors only go up to 350 Fahrenheit. But I reckon he went beyond that."

"What's going on?" Hunter managed to ask before his mouth gulped in a large amount of water. He swallowed, and immediately felt an expansion of pressure from his gut. His vampire physiology meant he no longer digested like a human, but he recognized what this most resembled - gas pressure - only a hundred times more intense and sharper than any pain he had ever had in his mortal life. He yelled out in agony. All the while, Hunter felt like he was beginning to float under a rapidly filling pool.

"How's the patient?" This voice, feminine and with a charming Welsh accent, rang bells with Hunter's memory. It was the voice of Dr. Ife Mwodim, a former Dallas Order agent, now spending her time on the west coast in a new department of the organization. He still couldn't see her – between the steam coming off his skin and the rapidly growing surface of the water he was beginning to thrash about in, there was too much in front of his eyes to allow him clear sight. Not to mention the pain in his stomach. He groaned again.

"He's melting all the ice," Slicer exclaimed.

"And he sounds like he's having a massive attack of indigestion," Mugan said, pointing out at the scene in front of them.

"Gents," Dr. Ife said to the two men flanking her, "I'd advise you to hit the deck."

Slicer, Mugan, and Ife clamored for the snow-lined ground and put their hands over their heads.

Hunter let out a tremendous belch, but as he did so, he felt his neck stretching unnaturally, his body shuddering as though resisting a transformation it didn't yet understand. There was a disturbing sensation, like something fluid and molten was coursing just beneath his skin, seeking release. His trachea extended and widened, his esophagus spasmed, and Hunter let out an expulsion of steam, followed by white-hot flame at a rate normally seen from a North Sea oil rig explosion.

The ball of flame coalesced and turned red and orange as it curled up the walls of the stone-walled cavern, dissipated into a cloud of jet-black smoke, and curled its way harmlessly to the ceiling several hundred feet above them all.

Hunter bobbed in the water, stunned, as the steam also began to thin out, allowing him to look at his surroundings. He was in a large crater of ice, at least 100 feet wide, and floating like a single piece of cork amongst the gently lapping waves.

"H-hello?" He asked, meekly, his voice bouncing off the ice crater and around the stone walls of the cavern. He could see there were industrial work lights illuminating the area.

"Hello there! Nice to see you again." Dr. Ife's cheerful greeting defied the sheer strangeness of the situation. From her side, she produced a large donut-shaped life preserver and tossed it as hard as she could. The buoy sailed across the crater and landed with a *plop* just shy of Hunter's reach. He paddled the extra few yards to grab hold of it.

"What... what just happened?" Hunter asked.

"That's what I'd like to know!" Slicer got up from the ground and joined Ife in looking over the precipice at Hunter. "This was solid ice not 30 seconds ago!"

"Simple," Ife said nonchalantly. "He melted the ice."

Slicer growled, "I'm not *stupid*, lady, I get that he melted the ice, but why is he getting hot enough to *melt* ice and not be a fiery pile of vampire ash?"

It was not an unfair question to ask, Hunter conceded. Floating there, he felt the water refreshing, almost calming. It was also slightly salty, reminding him of the time he once tried an all-saltwater isolation tank on a trip to Florida, but without the muggy atmosphere.

"It's the demon in him," Mugan explained, unzipping a large duffel bag from his side and pulling out a mass of yellow nylon rope. "It's trying to decide what element it wants to manifest."

Slicer ran a hand through his thick, knotted mane of black-and-grey hair. "You're losin' me, folks."

Exhausted, Hunter floated there in the massive pool and listened.

"Put simply, we know Hunter is part demon, but we don't know what *kind* of demon," Ife said, kneeling to help Mugan unknot the rope. "Hunter shows traits of several different kinds, and those traits are fighting among themselves for dominance."

"There are energy demons, you see," said Mugan as they worked. "Psychic, siphonic, chaos demons... probably dozens more. We're trying to learn about them as we encounter them. Er, could you grab a pair of spikes and a hammer from my bag?" Mugan gestured to Slicer, who acquiesced.

Draped over the flotation device, Hunter closed his eyes as he listened to the three chat about him, accompanied by the clink of hammer against metal.

"How did I let you talk me into this?" Kai asked from behind one bush.

"You said you wanted some insight into how Hunter and I procured blood!" Gibson whispered from a bush across the walking path from Kai.

"I thought you would just tell me," Kai countered.

"What good would that do you when you're hungry?"

Kai grunted. "I'm just... I don't like feeding on people when it's not justified."

"Maybe you'll get lucky and we'll witness a mugging," Gibson offered. Upon hearing some voices in the distance, he signaled for them to crouch behind the bushes.

Peering through the gaps in the foliage, Kai reasoned if nothing else, he could just watch Gibson. *And think about Hunter*, he added to himself. He hoped their partner was doing alright...

As the voices came nearer, Kai could hear they were from young, drunk men. Frat boys, perhaps, judging from their shirts emblazoned with college insignia. Four of them, chatting amongst each other with slurred, giggly speech patterns. One seemed to be straggling a few steps behind, fiddling with his phone.

Kai watched as Gibson began to slowly emerge from his hiding spot, his eyes fixed on the straggler. Gibson spoke softly, and in an exaggerated, almost cartoonish surfer's accent:

"Whoa, look at this fucked-up looking squirrel!"

The drunk young man spun on his heels. "What, really?" he murmured as he stumbled toward Gibson. Kai watched in amazement as the inebriated guy trotted right up to the bush like a puppy expecting a treat.

"Yeah, sure," Gibson said, his fangs already out. "I think he's got, like, webbed toes or some shit."

"Sweet," slurred the young man as he climbed right into the bush beside Gibson. It looked to Kai as if he switched on the camera function on his phone, hopeful to see some weird animal video footage. Kai emerged from his bush and cautiously scampered across the footpath. He reached the other bush and observed Gibson, his mouth attached hungrily to the frat boy's neck.

Dreamily, the man purred, "Mmm... Sheila?"

"You do look like you're enjoying the meal," Kai said. He nervously looked around the park area, but didn't see anyone nearby. The dude's friends were long gone.

Gibson nodded in response. Pulling himself from the neck of his victim, he licked his chops and fangs. "Perfectly delectable. Would you like to share?"

"Sharing is caring," the man underneath him giggled.

"Shh. You're less cute when you talk," Gibson chided, patting the man on the head, before tilting it towards Kai's direction.

Kai opened his mouth to say something, and was surprised to feel his fangs pop out. He could smell the young man's blood - so fresh and fervent, with a mixture of hormones and cheap beer wafting to his nostrils. He covered his mouth and shook his head.

"Very well," Gibson said. He gave his thumb a quick jab with a fang before letting his teeth revert back to normal. He smudged the bloody thumb over the fang marks on the man and watched the wounds heal. "I've got some reserve on hand at my place. You're welcome to that, and we can get comfy and chat some more before bed."

"What about him?"

Gibson rose from the ground and tilted the drunk and now considerably lighter-blooded man against the tree trunk behind them. "He'll be fine. Sunrise will wake him up. Either that or the sprinklers, whenever they" –

Before he could finish his sentence, the *psh-psh-psh-psh* of the landscaping sprinklers began, and the bush area became encased in a dome of spray. Gibson leaped up and onto the footpath next to Kai.

"... go off!" Gibson finished.

He and Kai stared at the frat boy as he slept happily amid the impromptu shower. Kai turned to Gibson and burst out laughing – a sight and sound that surprised Gibson... and caused him to begin laughing as well.

They walked down the footpath towards the parking lot, laughing jovially.

Hunter lifted his head from the life preserver. He felt he had been asleep for days, but it must have only been a few moments, because he could still hear Ife, Mugan, and Slicer chatting away.

"Alright, buckaroo," Slicer said from the crater's edge. With a kick, a rope ladder spilled over the side, reaching down to just at water level. "Time to get out of the pool."

Hunter lifted himself further from the plastic of the floating ring. There was a crackling noise that accompanied the movement of his arms. The icy cavern surroundings seemed to cling to him unnaturally. As he moved toward Slicer, an unsettling resistance, as though his very essence was merging with the water, sent a shiver through him.

"Guys," he shouted. "I can't move my legs."

Ife popped up beside Slicer. "What do you mean?"

"They're... frozen? I think?" Hunter was shifting his body in the water trying to illustrate his point. It felt, when he tried to kick one leg at a time, that both were moving. "I can't see for certain, the water's too dark!"

He also noticed the feeling of extreme heat he'd been saddled with for days was gone. Now he felt nothing but cold. His throat felt like he'd swallowed a mouthful of minty toothpaste. The icy water against his skin didn't feel entirely external; it was as if the cold were seeping inside him, dissolving something fundamental. His limbs didn't just freeze–they softened, almost yielding to the water around him.

"There's a collapsible raft by the lift doors," Ife said, her voice steady but urgent as she tapped Slicer on the shoulder. "Grab it, toss it over. Mugan – take my walkie, radio for assistance. We'll need help pulling four people out of this freezing ice bath!"

"Four?" Mugan asked, confused, grabbing the walkie off Dr. Ife's hip.

"We're going to have to go in and help young Hunter stay afloat."

"Help!" Hunter suddenly dipped below the surface of the water.

"Quickly, please!" Ife said before hoisting herself over the side of the crater, climbing down the rope ladder and dipping herself into the water.

By the time she did so, Slicer had run a half-football field's circumference and reached a metallic locker containing a collapsible raft. He pushed it over the side of the crater. Hearing the splash, he looked over the edge, saw Ife swimming toward the now-vacant life raft, and swan-dived into the water himself.

After radioing for help, Mugan climbed into the pool via the rope ladder. The water was bracing, causing instant pain, but he dutifully began to swim toward where Slicer was meeting Ife.

"On my count of three, dive and lift!" Ife shouted.

"One... two... three!"

Mugan continued to swim, fighting the urge to yell out at how uncomfortably cold the water was. He reached the collapsible raft and began to pop it into its usable form as Slicer and Ife resurfaced.

"Never mind that boat - give us a hand here!" Ife shouted before she took a deep breath and went back underwater, followed by Slicer. Mugan dove in after them.

A few seconds later, they popped back above the surface, along with a large, Hunter-shaped block of solid ice.

5
SPINE-CHILLER

Kai stood in shock as he stared into the closet, breathing in the distinctive smell of freshly-conditioned leather.

Gibson picked up on the stunned silence almost immediately. "Sounds like you went into the wrong cupboard," he called out from the kitchen. "I said the linens are in the one to the *right*."

"...Ah," was all Kai could manage. His eyes darted across the straps, studs, and loops, some adorned with metallic spikes and teeth. "I... I suppose I did."

As Kai remained frozen, Gibson approached and opened the actual linen cupboard. Pulling out a set of sheets, he remarked, "Some of those haven't been used yet. Hunter marveled at a few of those harnesses in San Francisco but couldn't decide on one, so I surprised him with the whole lot. I even got the cat o'nine tails he wanted me to use on him. The shop owners were quite pleased with the order."

Gibson stopped when he noticed Kai's rigid posture. "You... you seem disturbed," he said, tapping Kai on the shoulder.

"Not disturbed. I just... I didn't realize Hunter was into... that kind of thing," Kai replied hoarsely.

"You don't approve?"

Kai blinked. "It's not that. It's nothing he ever brought up with me," he muttered, trailing off into silence. "He's never even asked to bottom for me."

Gibson nodded and gently closed the closet door. "Well, let's get the sofa set up, shall we?"

In the living area, Kai pushed the glass coffee table aside as Gibson removed the sofa cushions and pulled out the mattress. They worked in unison to unfold the fitted sheet and secure it in place.

"You don't think less of Hunter for his interests, do you?" Gibson asked as he tucked the sheet over a corner.

"Certainly not!" Kai sounded offended. His tone softened. "I'm only..."

"Perhaps he senses it doesn't interest you?" Gibson suggested. "He's an empath, you know. Even without the demon lineage, he'd still have a knack for reading people. He probably knows it's not your thing and avoids making you uncomfortable."

Kai's face tightened, but he nodded thoughtfully. "Maybe."

Gibson clipped the sheet straps into place. "Hunter trusts you with his personal history, doesn't he? The sensitive parts?"

"He does," Kai admitted. "But I'm sure there's still stuff he's holding back."

"He does the same with me," Gibson said, his voice tinged with faint sadness. "He's open about the lighter stories but avoids anything painful. I've tried to invite those conversations, but he won't share."

Kai frowned. "That's surprising. I assumed he'd talk with you about that."

"No. But he knows I'm there if he needs to. It seems we complement him as partners. What he can't share with one of us, he does with the other. It's not about withholding; it's about balance."

Kai considered this. "Maybe he's still figuring out how to share all of himself between us."

Gibson offered his hand to help Kai off the floor. "Speaking of sharing, have you talked to him about... Kate?"

Kai sighed and sat on the corner of the sofa bed. "Not yet."

Gibson unfolded the duvet, glancing at Kai. "I assumed he'd have talked to you about the leather side of himself. You know, given how well you know each other."

Kai frowned. "We've shared a lot, but some things just haven't come up."

"Or maybe he thought you already knew. He's perceptive like that... like how he knew about your being pansexual before you ever mentioned it."

Kai froze, his hands hovering over the fabric. "He... knows?"

"Of course," Gibson said with a chuckle. "It's Hunter. He probably picked up on it the first time you met."

Kai's lips parted in disbelief. "I've been stressing about how to tell him, and he's just... known all along?"

Tears welled in his eyes, their green hue intensifying with sorrow.

Gibson placed a comforting hand on Kai's shoulder. "Your relationship hasn't been built on full disclosure, but you've always had understanding. Hunter wouldn't care about the gender of who you court, and you know that."

Kai's expression softened, the green receding from his eyes. "You're right."

"Whether he'll drop the macho facade long enough to admit that is another matter," Gibson said with a wry smile, fluffing the pillows as Kai let out a quiet laugh.

The team of Mugan, Slicer, and Ife shivered in the frigid water, struggling to keep the large block of ice containing Hunter afloat. Their breaths came in short bursts, misting in the icy air as they worked together, their movements deliberate and desperate.

Mugan leaned closer to the ice, squinting. "Where the hell is he?"

Ife shifted her weight, trying to get a better view. "I think... I think he metamorphosed," she said, her voice tight with exertion.

"What?" Mugan asked sharply.

Before Ife could elaborate, a burst of activity from above drew their attention. A rescue team of six agents appeared at the edge of the water pit, clad in bright DayGlo yellow jackets and grey balaclavas. They moved with practiced efficiency, setting up a pulley system.

"Pulley's coming down!" one of them called, tossing a red belt toward the group.

As the belt hit the water, Ife glanced at the ice block. Frost thickened rapidly, creeping like a living thing. "He turned into liquid," she said, her words hurried. "He must have frozen in that state. It's... elemental demon behavior."

"Great," Mugan muttered, grabbing the belt. "I'll dive under and secure it. Can you get on top of the block?"

"Boost me," Ife said. Mugan crouched, forming a step with his hands. Ife placed her foot in his grip, and with a powerful push, he launched her onto the ice. She landed with a grunt, pulling the strap over the block and fastening it into place.

Meanwhile, Slicer groaned and pushed himself away from the ice. He curled into a ball, his body convulsing. Ife and Mugan, distracted, nearly lost control of the block again. As they struggled to stabilize it, Slicer swam to the wall of the pit. Long, pale claws emerged from his hands as grey fur sprouted across his body. With a guttural growl, he climbed the icy wall, digging into it with his transformed limbs.

Mugan resurfaced and shouted, "The belt's secure! Pull us up!" The pulley system groaned as the team above began hoisting the ice block. Ife clung to the straps, her knuckles white.

Mugan launched himself out of the water with a vampire's strength, landing lightly beside the rescue team. He watched as the block was set on solid ground, Ife jumping off just as it touched down.

Nearby, Slicer's coyote form twisted and contorted, fur retracting as he shifted back into his human shape. Mugan stared, wide-eyed. "Have you never encountered a lycanthrope before?" Ife asked, nudging him.

Mugan shook his head, still watching as Slicer's human form stabilized. A rescue worker handed Slicer a thermal blanket, which he accepted with a muttered "Cheers."

"Are you... alright?" Mugan asked awkwardly.

Slicer's nose twitched, and he sniffed the air. His head snapped toward the ice block. "Something's wrong," he said.

"A lot of things are wrong," Mugan quipped.

"Shh," Ife hissed. "Slicer, what do you smell?"

"Fire," Slicer replied, his voice low.

The team turned to the ice block. Frost melted rapidly, condensation dripping as an ominous orange glow emanated from within. The block began to crack.

"Squad!" Ife barked. "Surround it!"

The rescue team moved in, but they were too late. With a deafening crack, the ice shattered. Flames erupted, and Hunter emerged, fully nude and wreathed in red, curling fire. He roared, the sound piercing and inhuman, a mix of fury and anguish.

Before anyone could react, Hunter lunged at the nearest crew member, his hand morphing into talons. He slashed at the man's face, leaving deep gashes rimmed with scorched flesh.

"Fuckin' hell," Slicer growled, dropping his blanket. In an instant, he shifted back into his coyote form and charged, slamming into Hunter with full force. Hunter toppled backward, stunned.

Mugan was already at the injured crew member's side, examining his wounds. "What's your name, mate?" he asked, his voice steady.

"Trevor," the man murmured, his eyes glazed from shock.

"You'll be alright, Trevor," Mugan said, pressing gauze to the wounds. Blood trickled from the cuts, along with a faint orange fluid. His eyes narrowed.

Meanwhile, Slicer had reformed into his human body, his glowing blue eyes fixed on Hunter. As if caught in a spell, Hunter froze. The flames enveloping him dissipated, revealing his unmarred skin. His tattoo glowed the same icy blue as Slicer's eyes.

Hunter's breath came in ragged puffs of smoke. "I c-can't take this anymore," he choked out, his voice breaking. "Somebody... please kill me."

6
TIPPING POINT

After making slow progress on their trek northward, Olivia got word from a passing camp that the Evansville, Indiana area was noted as a vampire-friendly hub. While still a young city by 1901 standards - it had only been incorporated for 60 years or so - it was growing rapidly, with train depots operating round-the-clock. The outlying farm areas were thriving. Olivia reckoned they could travel to Evansville, stay a week or so, restock their supplies (and of course find enough blood to keep them well-satiated), then head on the final leg of their journey toward Canada.

Ever since the group agreed on this plan, there had been very little dissent or negative word from William. It seemed as though even he could see light at the end of the proverbial tunnel. Perhaps once in Indiana, they could board a train to take them directly to Ontario. When he brought up the idea, he, for the first time since Caeden had met William, sounded enthusiastic about something.

Indeed, when they reached Evansville, they found more activity and signs of human life than they had in ages. Streets were bustling the evening they arrived with pedestrians and horse-drawn buggies. It was easy to walk about at night and blend in with the locals, and easy for them to stop in at various storefronts to buy new clothes and supplies. Even though Caeden had nary a penny to his name, Olivia was more than generous with him, getting him a new set of shirt and trousers to replace his worn and permanently dirt-stained wardrobe.

While they stayed at a boarding house on the city's northern edge, Olivia did more investigating about the area. She learned there were miles of farmhouses growing out from all sides of the city.

"I wanted to propose something to you all," she said the following night. "What would you all say towards ending our travels here, now?"

"Why for?" Spencer asked. "I thought we were all set on Canada?"

"Well, that's still an option," Olivia said. "But, this area seems quite nice, too. It seems rather feasible, and certainly affordable, to make a home off any of the main roads leading from town. And there are plenty of farms we could use when we need to take blood."

"I saw some of those farmsteads," William said, stirring from the bed he was already tucked into. "We could even start a farm, make a little money off the crops... and animals, too, instead of just... feeding off 'em."

After a unanimous vote, the very next evening, Olivia set about securing a parcel of land near a creek, surrounded on either side by young oak trees. Behind the spot of land where the home would be built stood a vast acreage of land, rich in grass with just a few foothills...

and not a human to be found anywhere nearby. The border of the town was five miles from the road. They had found their new home.

Working with a proxy who didn't question why she couldn't conduct business in the daytime, Olivia secured the homestead. From that point, things accelerated: Olivia and Spencer were able to find night jobs, the earnings from which went straight into paying for the real estate; meanwhile, William and Caeden set to work on building a house.

William, having retained memories of his carpenter's apprenticeship, guided Caeden in clearing plots, foundation work, cutting lumber, and building fences. Much to everyone's surprise, William complimented Caeden's handiwork on several occasions.

Soon, walls were hoisted, rooms were connected, a sturdy roof was installed, and the humble building was complete. The nest finally had a place to call their own. It was simple construction, certainly, but it was equipped for their purposes, and everyone had their place in it – Olivia had a room to herself, and the men shared the other large bed quarters. There was also a quaint kitchen complete with a stovepipe-style oven, though it was going to mainly be used for heating only. There were windows, but each one was built with oversize shutters that could be latched in place during the daylight hours.

After move-in, William went out each night for two weeks in search of employment; he eventually secured a job as night patrol officer for a large dairy farm about 12 miles from the house.

Spencer then ended his temporary job and stayed at the farmstead, digging a small garden he could manage himself. The intent was to grow a small amount of vegetables to start with, enough to take in a few hand baskets to sell at the city's market square at night. Caeden volunteered to help with the project, and he and Spencer would work together in tilling, planting seeds, and eventually, harvesting.

During their hours together, Caeden would notice Spencer getting deliberately close as they worked. A hand would brush against his every so often; a booted foot would clunk up against his during breaks. Every time their bodies connected in some way, however innocently, Caeden would feel the same strange sensation race through his body.

The sensation was one of happiness, adoration, and fear, all blended together. Some mornings, as he lay awake in bed, he would worry whether his feelings for Spencer, whatever they turned out to be, were the right or wrong things to be feeling. He knew, without any shadow of a doubt, that his desire to be with another man was simply natural to him.

One morning, rather than this parade of confused thoughts, he had a realization that his deeply rooted fear, the thing keeping him from acting on any romantic impulse he now knew he was harboring, was about what would happen to him – or Spencer – if William were to find out about it. After all, it had been a tremendous effort just to get to the point where William accepted Caeden into the nest to begin with. Even then, it never seemed like the two could speak about anything on a deep level. Caeden couldn't even picture what would happen if William didn't realize feelings were developing between Caeden and Spencer and then discovered the two embracing. Or even more.

Or even more? Caeden, for the first time, had let his imagination spread. Until now, when he thought about Spencer, or pictured them together, it was benign imagery: holding hands, sleeping side-by-side, and memories of their night in the lake. But suddenly, Caeden also began imagining pressing his lips against Spencer's, tasting him, feeling his arms go further down than just to the waist.

He had just began picturing what Spencer might feel like, intimately, when Caeden forced himself away from the thought. He was still far too young, he told himself. He was still getting the hang of being a well-behaved vampire to let a same-sex relationship enter the equation.

Olivia, meanwhile, had taken it upon herself to go out past the creek and into an area of unclaimed land to hunt. Fresh blood, if drained from the animal or human, and into a container, was viable and nutritious for only an hour or two, but it could be done. Once a week, she would take Caeden along with her to learn her methodology.

With a varied number of animal species in this area compared with the South, she also allowed him to sample other specimens directly. Anytime they came across a new animal, she would let Caeden know so he could remember each animal's behavior, flavor profile, and texture of their blood.

Larger animals lurking closer to the hills required certain cajoling before the vampires could taste. On one trek, Olivia taught Caeden how to use his ability to charm a target in order to hypnotize them, allowing him to feed without objection or a fight.

"You look into their eyes," she said. "It's all in the eyes. Animals, though they do not speak like you or me, can still be comforted through the most basic of psychic bonds... and that bond is formed in the stare. Simply think what it is you want them to know, in this case, they are helping you stay fed, and that they will come to no harm... and they will quickly understand."

The animal, in this case, was a brown bear, lumbering slowly a few hundred yards away. With Olivia's guidance, Caeden slowly approached the bear. They slouched a bit so the bear wouldn't immediately think it was being attacked. The young cub, probably a few years old, noticed Caeden, cocking its head quizzically.

Sensing this was his moment of opportunity, Caeden focused his mind on the message he wanted to convey - control, comfort, and ultimately, food.

He began to sense his eyes widening, and a soft yellow glow began to emanate from the borders of his field of vision.

"You're nervous," Olivia said. "Take a few moments to calm yourself. You will sense when you're ready to proceed."

Caeden nodded. Still staring at the bear, he counted a few numbers off in his head. The glow in his vision changed from yellow to green. The bear, still looking at

Caeden, sat on its hindquarters. Its eyes slowly began to change from black to the same shade of green.

Contact.

"Hi there, little fella," he said aloud. He knew he didn't really need to speak, but he figured Olivia would want to know what he was thinking. "Bet you're surprised to see me. But don't you worry - I won't be here long. And I'm not here to hurt you; I just need a little bit of your blood, then I can be on my way. It won't take but a moment, and you won't be in any danger or in any pain. I promise."

Caeden watched in surprise as the small bear closed its eyes and laid down, craning its neck out. It was as if the bear went into immediate hibernation. With Olivia nodding her approval, Caeden stepped cautiously and knelt by the bear's body. He could see the area on its neck where he should bite. He let his fangs descend, and with a skyward look, wishing himself luck, he bit down. He took three small, quick pulls from the bear's neck before lifting his head again.

"Wow," he said, licking his chops, shivering slightly. "That's really sweet."

"I expected it would be," Olivia said, approaching them and whispering softly. "There's likely a hive of honeybees nearby. I can smell the slightest hint of clover blossom on his fur." She knelt down to take a sip herself, then pierced her thumb, drawing the bloody digit over the fang marks they had caused. The four holes filled in with a dark viscous material before forming a skin, then fur. The bite marks were completely gone, Caeden marveled.

The sugar in the bear's blood immediately began to metabolize in his body and heighten Caeden's other senses. He looked up at the moon, which seemed brighter than just a few minutes before. He swore he could feel the moonbeams' energy hitting his skin, dissolving and absorbing into his arms. It felt amazing.

His eyes darted from side to side, and like a child experiencing his first high from a chocolate bar, Caeden took in every detail of his surroundings – the lush green hue of the grass under his feet, the texture of each blade, even through his shoes! A clacking of antlers some distance away made him snap his attention to the far right from where he was standing.

He could see two male deer running off, away from him.

Caeden's stomach tensed and a hot sensation flushed over him. His skin began to tingle; a disturbing, prickly heat. Oh no, he realized, recognizing the sensation rapidly building. Rogue intuition was forcing its way through his body. He tried to talk himself down off this steep ledge, but he felt himself falling forward with abandon.

The pulsating of his energy drowning out the protests of Olivia, Caeden spun in the direction of the fleeing deer and took off with blinding speed. Already at top strength, he flew towards the animals. Fueling a growing hunger was the thought of how satisfying it would feel to tackle one of these creatures, attacking it ruthlessly, rending its flesh, digging his hands into its entrails, draining its body of every last drop of life, and tossing the body aside – maybe against a tree - like a rag doll.

The mental imagery only served to make him run faster. He didn't even realize his tongue was hanging rabidly out of his mouth. Within seconds he was in reaching distance of the deer.

With an otherworldly snarl, Caeden wrapped a hand around the antlers of one of the young bucks. He yanked. He pulled so hard the antler actually broke in his grasp. Tossing it behind him, Caeden took both arms and snatched the animal, bucking and writhing, lifting it a few inches off the ground as it barked in a panic.

Caeden felt his fingernails turn into claws - nearly talons - and he cruelly dug his fingers deep into the deer's flesh. The animal howled, and Caeden slammed them both to the ground, using his weight to pin the deer underneath him. Fangs fully extended once more, he snarled and dove for the wounded creature's neck. He slurped and gurgled as he let out a frenzied scream into the blood gushing into his mouth.

"STOP THIS NOW!"

Caeden heard Olivia's command as she caught up to the melee. She sped up as she neared the distressed animal and attempted to peel Caeden off of it.

Unfortunately, he was now over the precipice. Fully enraged, he snarled and without taking his eyes off the deer's throat, whipped his forearm into Olivia's face, backhanding her out of his way. She let out a surprised yell as she crashed against the trunk of a tree some distance away.

Filled with unbridled, unprovoked, unexplained anger, Caeden savored the taste of the deer as he drank mouthful after mouthful. It had been petrified in these last moments – and he could taste that fear across each taste bud. He had caused this fear, he realized, and the reward was the blood, sending sparks through every synapse in his body.

It made him crave more, he realized, as the final ounce of blood emptied into his mouth. Remembering the impulse he had moments before, he gripped the dead animal by the scruff of its neck, and with a mighty roar, hurled it in Olivia's direction. She barely scrambled away before the deer's body landed with a heavy thud against the tree.

More. The thought repeated through his body. All thoughts that might have held him back - the pain he undoubtedly caused the wretched deer - the trouble this will cause his nest mates - even the thought that his actions now would assuredly ruin anything he had going with Spencer - were drowned out by the sheer evil tone of the thoughts pounding in his eardrums. *I must have MORE.*

Caeden bolted off into the trees, on a quest to find the other deer that had escaped. In a matter of just a few seconds, he caught sight of the survivor, and his vision narrowed. Now with extreme focus on this second deer, Caeden felt his anger growing exponentially. Every second that passed without this deer in his grasp, he was a failure. He was a superior being, damn it.

But as he flew closer to the deer, his psyche tried to plead with him for control. His brain fired off memories from that first dreadful night as a newborn vampire, and how he flew away from his sire's burning house, how he saw the band of mob members hunting for him.

Why did this happen to him?

The hopelessness of the situation only served to make Caeden madder, and his already focused eyesight became washed in a nearly-blinding tinge of red light.

Before the haze took over, Caeden was smacked in the face, the sudden and forceful nature of the blow knocking him back and crashing him to the ground. With a growl, he squinted his coal-red eyes to get a glimpse of his attacker.

Spencer.

Armed with a spare platen of wood from the farmhouse, Spencer stood over Caeden. His eyes were glowing just as brightly as Caeden's, but instead of red, the color of Caeden's rage, Spencer's eyes were a dazzling, polar ice-like shade of blue. Spencer said nothing, but bore his stare deep into Caeden's eyes.

Underneath him, Caeden stared back, transfixed. He tried to blink, but by then the connection had been made. Caeden began to feel the flow of psychic energy into his body. A calming aura enveloped him, and he began to hear Spencer as he spoke to Caeden telepathically, muddled and muffled as Caeden's rogue rage continued to fight for control.

You must accept things as they are, Spencer intoned. *It's okay. I am here, and I care. I care about you and your well-being.*

The words 'I care' echoed, reverberating off the walls in Caeden's brain. Combined with the soothing aura flowing through him, Caeden was able to shake his head free of the haze of anger and the thirst to kill.

Spencer knelt over Caeden, his arms extended as if tenting his body over Caeden's form. He waited for a sign that all was normal again.

Olivia trudged toward them, sounding tired and haggard as she spoke. "I thought we had drummed all this out of you," she said sadly. She motioned for Spencer to move aside. This allowed Caeden to sit upright. Rather that stand, he stayed on the ground, sitting cross-legged in the dirt.

He sighed in agitation. "I'm sorry!" Caeden began to cry. "I'm sorry, I truly am. Once it starts, its just so hard to get it to stop."

"The only answer is to try harder," Olivia said. Her matronly tone was gone; her voice sported the edge of a mother grown tired of constantly retying her child's shoes for him. "You won't get much farther in this life – or in this nest – if you snap like this again. What do you think with happen if you flew into a rage like this in the town square? How could we possibly explain you?

"For our benefit, as well as your own," she said, "you must find a way to permanently control these outbreaks and stop yourself before something goes drastically and irretrievably wrong."

Without another word, Olivia turned and began walking back toward their home.

Caeden sat there on the ground, blood beginning to stream from the corners of his eyes. He felt a loud sob growing; he covered his mouth before it let out.

Spencer knelt beside Caeden, close to tears himself. "Hey," he said after a few moments. "Walk with me." He stood upright and held out his hand. After a brief hesitation, Caeden took the hand and stood. They began walking, towards the farm but at a different angle than Olivia, allowing them continued privacy.

"I feel like I'm back at the county schoolhouse," Caeden said. "No matter how hard I struggle to learn, and no matter how well I think I am doing, Teacher is still ultimately disappointed in me. And that's Olivia," he added, kicking pebbles as they crossed his path. "William still treats me like a bastard child he didn't sign up to look after."

Spencer sighed. "You do understand though, that rogue vampires *are* bastards, quite literally? They're born from a lack of compassion on their sire's part."

Caeden rubbed his temples. "Yes, of course I know," he groaned. "But I'm *trying* is the point. Really, I am."

"You are," Spencer confirmed. "I reckon it's gonna be a lifelong thing. You'll always have this tiny part of you that wants to lose control and destroy. It's going to take greater-than-human strength and will to overcome. But remember: you already *are* greater-than human."

They walked down to the riverbank, watching the water glisten as it flowed under the moonlight. As they talked, Spencer turned Caeden so that his back was to him. He placed his hands on Caeden's shoulders and began gently rubbing them.

It relaxed Caeden and allowed him enough energy to begin pouring his feelings out.

"All I ever wanted was to leave a legacy," Caeden said. "I joined the war effort because I thought, even if I didn't live long, I could die with honor. But now, look at me. I'm this... *creature*, created out of an evil action. And I'm battling to keep hold of my own humanity. I'm in another war, and I was on the wrong side of the war to start with."

Spencer let his arms sink down, but he made a conscious effort to wrap Caeden in a hug as he spoke. "I can't begin to imagine what it must all feel like for you," he said. "I know you didn't ask to be put in the position you're in now. But if it helps at all... I'm glad you are here."

The words seemed to stun Caeden. "You do?"

"Truly." Spencer hugged Caeden to his chest. "I think about you more than I should probably admit. When I heard you yell out tonight, I worried about you. I worried *for* you. I want to do what I can to help you, and to protect you."

"I don't know what to say..." Caeden turned to look at Spencer.

"Perhaps we don't need to say anything?" Spencer leaned closer to Caeden. Their lips began to part as they inched nearer.

A noise from the wooded area on the opposite side of the creek made them both break the near-kiss and look in that direction. Caeden spotted a pair of eyes glisten in the moonlight. He was able to pinpoint the direction the noise was moving and he took off toward it, breaking free of Spencer's tender grip in the process.

Caeden knew he was in control of his own faculties because he didn't feel the prickly heat wash over him as he had earlier. He wasn't hunting to kill this time – at least, to start with. He was hunting for an identity, looking to see who had just been spying on them.

He bounded from one side of the creek to the other in one leap. Once his feet made contact with the other side, he crouched, then leapt for the nearest tree. He clamored up to a high, sturdy limb and scanned the area around him.

In a natural clearing between two groups of trees, Caeden could see a figure cloaked entirely in black, running as fast as it could. It seemed to be human; it wasn't running as fast as Caeden or his nest mates could. He considered running after the figure again, but stopped himself from doing so. No one was hurt, he reasoned, and the figure was leaving the area.

But he couldn't shake the fact that the figure seemed to have been watching Caeden and Spencer. But that could be dealt with at another time – if it needed to at all.

Spencer met Caeden as he hopped down from the tree. "What was that?"

"Don't know," Caeden replied. "There's not much time to worry about it," he said. "We ought to be getting back."

The mile or so back to the property were mostly spent in silence, but once they reached the fence outside the perimeter of their home, Caeden chose to speak. "I can't deny any longer," he said. "I think about you all the time, Spencer."

They looked into each other's eyes.

"You don't *have* to," Spencer replied, "but if you felt like it, I really would love to kiss you."

This shouldn't happen, Caeden warned himself. But again, he felt an urge he failed to withhold. He reached for Spencer, and made contact with his shoulders. Caeden pulled him close. They stood in this position for several minutes, before they finally moved their heads toward each other and met upon the lips.

For a fleeting moment, Caeden felt safe, and comfortable, and loved. His spirit began to soar–

–Until William's large, calloused hands clasped around Caeden's throat.

"What in the hell do you think you're up to?" William's voice had gotten so deep in his anger that it came out as a bare whisper. His fangs were out and his eyes a blaze of red.

Caeden struggled to answer, but William's grip closed off his vocal cords. He rasped feebly. William ignored Spencer's pleas for him to stop. Instead, he slammed Caeden to the ground.

"Is it not enough that I have to put up with your bouts of rage?" William seethed. "But now I come home to find you trying to corrupt my brother? You despicable piece of" –

"William! Please, stop this!" Spencer begged. "He was only... we were just"–

"Get back in the house."

"Damn it, William, you are not my maker and I am not a child." Spencer's voice was rigid and clipped. Caeden could hear in his voice that Spencer had been fighting to use those words for some time, and was only now pushed to use them.

William, still holding Caeden off the ground by the throat, slowly turned his head to look at Spencer. "I am your Elder, by bond and by breed. As your Elder, I *order* you back into the house!"

Propelled by the supernatural forces tying brethren vampires to one another, Spencer emitted a short cry as he was invisibly pushed back a few feet. He tried feebly to dig his heels into the ground and fight the command off, but he stumbled and continued walking backwards. Caeden caught Spencer mouthing the words, "I'm so very sorry, Caeden," before running back to the house at top speed.

Though he was not struggling for oxygen, the sheer force of William's strength upon his voice box was becoming intolerable. He was simply too strong to fight. Caeden dangled there, forced to listen to William's next words.

"I heard what happened out there," William murmured. His words were stern and deliberately chosen. "You've had forty years, four damn *decades* to fix yourself and you still can't stop it. Olivia may be willing to spend our eternity trying to turn you into something you are not. That's one thing. But when you try to seduce my brother, that is just one step too far."

Caeden's feet suddenly touched the ground, only to begin dragging back into the wooded area he and Spencer had just come from. He tried once again to wrench himself clear from William's grip, and failed. His field of vision began to blur, and then Caeden began to see a green light from around his eyes, a signal of panic which made him panic all the more.

Once in the thick of the woods, William tossed Caeden aside, watching him land and roll across the ground.

His head knocked against a tree trunk. Wincing, Caeden stirred, propping himself against the trunk. In front of him stood William, scowling and red-eyed. Beyond William was the tree where he had just laid waste to the deer, its body still piled lifelessly against another tree.

"You... are to stay away from him," William growled. "Do you understand me, you filth?" His eyes squinted down at Caeden as if he were pinpointing an insect crawling on some food. "Stay away from him. Stay away from us. Go find the nest of rogues you so obviously need to traipse around with. Fornicate with them for all I care. Be with your own kind."

William performed an about-face and began walking away. Without turning to address him again, William added:

"If I even *sense* you rising from that spot... I will kill you."

Shattered, both in bone and in spirit, Caeden lay there against the tree trunk, staring at the deer's body a few dozen yards away from him. He held back a cry of agony and shame for a few brief moments, but it was a losing battle. Even as his bones healed with each passing second, and he regained the ability to move, Caeden simply stayed in position, his soft cries turning into sobs, growing louder and louder. He spent the next hour writhing on the ground, delirious with sorrow. His fists clenched, pounding at the dirt, Caeden wailed. He had let his feelings, his urges, his affections get the better of him, and now he was paying the price. Again. Banished. Again. Alone and frightened of what was to come.

Again.

Caeden groaned as his body tensed. His energy had been nearly completely depleted, but the sun was close to rising. He had to make his way deeper into the woods and bury himself soon. He forced himself to stand, and in between muscle contractions from sobbing, trudged into the path leading into the forest.

7
LAKE EFFECT FOG

"Don't be silly," Ife said as she gently patted Hunter's shoulders. He was still in a state of distress, repeatedly saying that he wanted to die–permanently. "You do not need to be killed. This is just a stage you're going through. You'll come through it just fine!" She was doing her best to maintain a professional demeanor – but was failing.

She sympathized with the young vampire/cambion. In such a short span of time, Hunter and his body had undergone so much change and trauma: First vampirism, then a demonic puberty. With so little known information to go on regarding the latter, it was hard to determine how that was affecting the former. Just the same, she realized and understood that his extreme temperature changes, to say nothing of developing pure ice and fire from within his body, was draining both his energy level and his will to endure.

A biting and bracing wind was spraying their faces with wet snow. Each new fleck of snow that hit Hunter felt like a dart, its tip hitting a pore, a fresh new reminder that he caused a lot of pain to an innocent.

"Did I do a lot of damage to that crew member I attacked?" Hunter sniffed, trying not to break down.

"He has some pretty deep slash marks to his face," Mugan reported as he approached the station wagon parked outside the cavern. The back hatch was open, and Ife and Hunter had been sitting on the ledge to talk. "They'll heal in time. But Hunter," he paused, not wanting to add onto his troubles. "He's got some sort of poison in his blood."

"Poison?" Ife echoed.

"He has another fluid coming out of his wounds," Mugan explained. "It's very faint, but it's there. Something orange in color. He says it's causing the cuts to sting in a way uncommon than they should normally feel."

"Venom," Hunter sighed, wincing his eyes shut, knowing at once what Mugan was describing. He wished this ongoing nightmare would simply *end*. "It's got to be venom."

Opening his eyes to a confused face from Ife, Hunter explained. "During that last major investigation – remember, the alternate world, my doppelgänger, the dehydrated bodies? – We learned that demons can mark victims with a traceable venom. Those of us with demonic backgrounds can smell it. It weakens their bodies... and makes it easier to consume them."

Hunter shuddered, recalling the times they had witnessed a twinkish-looking man with demon lineage unhinge his jaws much like a snake, in order to eat the bodies - or at least parts - of humans whole.

Ife rubbed her chin. "I really have been out of the loop since I relocated to California," she mused. "Mugan, what more do you know about this?"

"Nothing more than that, I'm afraid," was Mugan's reply. "We've been trying to figure out how it manifests before Hunter developed the ability to produce it. I have to assume it came from those claws."

"The claw tips, to be precise," said a crisp voice from within the cavern. The trio turned their heads to see a woman emerge, striding confidently toward them. Her black suit was immaculately tailored, the polished shoes crunching over the snow with a deliberate rhythm. Her hair, tied in a severe bun, gave her an air of calculated precision.

"Kate Coupland, Ward 12's Gulf Coast division. Based out of Galveston," she introduced herself, extending a hand to Ife. Her tone was polite but clipped, carrying the cadence of someone accustomed to authority.

"Dr. Ife Mwodim. Ward 2 - General Manager of the Housing Rehabilitation Center in San Francisco," Ife replied, shaking her hand. "Before that, I was the lead medical examiner for the Dallas bureau."

"Of course," Kate said, releasing Ife's hand with practiced ease. "Mugan, I met you briefly down in South Padre Island." She gave him a curt nod before her gaze shifted to Hunter. Her brown eyes seemed to linger a second too long. "And Hunter–very nice to see you again."

Hunter nodded, his mind too clouded to process the interaction. "Ms. Coupland."

Kate's lips twitched into a professional smile, her gaze holding a glint of something sharper. "I was called in to advise after leading research into the siphonic demon we encountered at the beach. I have information to share. Shall we relocate back into the facility?"

Ife glanced at Hunter, noting his exhaustion. "Let's get you settled first, chuck." She helped him slide down from the station wagon's cargo bed, still wrapped in the crinkling foil sheet. Mugan joined her, each taking an arm as they guided him toward the cavern entrance.

Kate walked ahead, her heels clicking sharply against the icy ground.

Hunter, through the haze of his thoughts, frowned slightly. There was something familiar yet foreign in the set of her shoulders, though he couldn't quite place it.

Back at The Order's Dallas headquarters, in Kai's tastefully-decorated office, Gibson laid out and opened a dozen folders across Kai's desk, each containing various amounts of documents and photographs.

He was getting Kai up to speed on what he and Hunter had discovered up to that point on their assigned mission. "About a month ago, Houston police stopped a truck that had been smuggling in various drugs – cocaine concealed in suitcases, that sort of thing," Gibson explained. He pointed to a photo directly in front of Kai. It showed an opened cardboard box filled with test tubes - at least a hundred in number. "This was the odd one out. Their labs couldn't detect any sort of narcotic substance when they tested it. So, as is routine, they contacted us and arranged a transfer so we could test for anything supernatural or otherwise."

"And?" Kai asked, his fingers tented in front of his mouth as he listened to Gibson's report.

"It never made it to Dallas," Gibson said. "The courier made it to the drop point empty-handed. He was brought in and questioned but had absolutely no explanation for why he was there or what he was supposed to have delivered. It was like that information had been surgically removed from his memory."

"Any guesses as to what is in those tubes?" Kai pored over the photo. "Or who sent it?"

"The police photograph is too blurry to enhance," Gibson said. "Have you noticed that? It's well into the 21st century, yet mugshots and other police photographs are so low-resolution these days."

"Gibson, focus," Kai said calmly.

Gibson blinked. "Right. Um, no clear evidence, but you can sort of tell there's a marking on the caps of the test tubes." He indicated with his finger. "Five will get you ten that's some sort of Crown indicator."

The Crown was an interconnected group of underworld criminals. Sometimes their efforts were noticeable to the general public – an explosion or collapse of a prominent building, for example. Other times their activities were known only to those within The Order and was the group's chief reason for centuries of existence.

When Kai first met Hunter, his eventual partner and lover had been working for what turned out to be a Crown-operated company called InnerCore. While claiming to be creating technology to aid in medical research,

InnerCore's head of medical technology had in fact developed a piece of nanotech – a microscopically-small device whose transmitted radio waves could alter human cells.

A little more than a year later, when investigating the dwindling of the homeless population in the San Francisco area, Kai, Hunter, and Gibson (who had by this time defected from The Crown) discovered that these people had been kidnapped and experimented upon. Aided by a demon who could transverse planes of existence, the experiments had been hidden within an alternate version of the city. People had been transformed into mutated versions of all sorts of animals and insects... from walking crocodiles to hornets that could stand on two legs, and every conceivable combination in between.

What disturbed the investigators most during that case, was that for every single living person they had found hidden in that laboratory, there were three or four that had not survived the experimentation. Corpses had been stacked like cordwood against the walls, with no regard to who the people were or where they came from.

Kai remembered during his report from Ife, who had examined the bodies both living and dead during that incident, that a certain substance, which she only described as a 'serum,' had been found in the victims' bloodstream.

"There is a possibility," Kai said to Gibson, "that these test tubes contain more of this so-called 'serum.' But we must get proof."

"We should reach out to our Houston-area team to make sure they get their hands on more of this stuff," Gibson offered. "If it is indeed being trafficked, there's sure to be more."

"Until we get more solid evidence, there's at least two more people I need to reach out to," Kai said, opening a laptop that had been waiting to the left side of his desk. He began typing at a frenetic pace. "The first person will be Noah."

Noah Frank. One of Kai's closest friends for decades, Noah had volunteered to construct The Order's first multi-dimensional office in the other-world version of Dallas.

"Who's the other contact?" Gibson began filing the documents back into their folders.

Kai paused before responding. "The other Hunter."

Gibson bristled.

"I know, I know," Kai said before Gibson had a chance to open his mouth. "You'd rather not – but he's our only solid connection to life on the other side."

Gibson pursed his lips. He knew Kai was absolutely right. But ever since the alternate-world version of Hunter tried to seduce him – *in my own bed, no less*, Gibson seethed silently – he wanted nothing to do with him. Despite being an exact duplicate of the Hunter they knew and loved in every physical way, there was a smarminess, a beyond-the-pale arrogance that turned Gibson off. Likely a result of being a rock star, he assumed. Hunter II headed up a band dubbed the *Daywalkers*. From what little he had seen and heard, they *were* quite talented... for performing only cover songs.

The duplicate Hunter's bandmate was a lanky, blond little piece of shit too, who tried to kill the version of Hunter that Kai and Gibson were attached to. Frankly, Gibson thought, he could do without meeting either of them ever again. Still...

Gibson sighed. "I suppose if the other Hunter could give us more of an education into how this serum works, it would be a blessing," he said.

"This would also give us a chance to make sure Noah's doing alright," Kai said, opening up the email client on his computer and typing off a quick message. "I'll let him know we plan to visit. I'll also take care of reaching out to the other Hunter," he added, hoping Gibson realized the gesture he was trying to make with the offer.

Then Kai's watch beeped, and he looked at it. "Date time," he said absently as he made a few firm taps on his computer's trackpad. "If you can, see if you can get any info on other trafficking busts down along the coast," Kai requested. "Cross reference what was found at each scene against what was stored into evidence. Maybe there's a pattern of other material going missing."

"Aye-aye, cap'n," Gibson said, flicking his mane of sleek black hair over his left shoulder. He sat in Kai's plush black leather sofa and took out his phone, tapping the screen with his thumb.

"How much of my time is going to be spent in medical wards?" Hunter's question went unanswered. He watched as Mugan, Ife, and Kate murmured among themselves in a tight huddle in front of his hospital bed.

He fiddled with the IV tubing stuck into his left wrist and jiggled the bag it was attached to. "I'm a biker now, you know," he said. After a moment of continued non-response from the group, he added, "I think I'm going to get jumped into the gang soon. I think I could manage a few more knives to the gut. Make it a biannual tradition."

Still nothing.

"I'm seriously tired of this shit," Hunter growled, the voice not in step with his usual demeanor. That made the group turn their heads.

"I'm sorry, Hunter," Mugan said. "We're trying to figure out the best way to help you. It's a bit of a puzzle when we don't know what to expect."

"You've been able to expel both freezing energy and flame energy," Ife said, taking a spot on the other side of the gurney opposite Hunter as the three approached. "We don't know if that's expected behavior or if one type may overtake the other."

"I told them we're under no rush," Kate said, her soft and demure voice adding to the mix a comforting sensation for Hunter. "They've suggested that what might be best for you is to take a 24-hour sabbatical."

"Meaning knock me out," Hunter said, gesturing to the bag of Evermore being fed through the tubes.

"You could certainly use a deep sleep," Mugan said, turning the nozzle at the neck of the IV drip to begin the flow of fluid. Hunter watched the tube slowly, slowly fill with the red synthetic blood, inching its way to his wrist. "This'll replenish the nutrients and vitamins you've lost with your... elemental changes – and I added in a sedative. You should wake up at this time tomorrow quite refreshed!"

Hunter took a deep sigh, observing the Evermore snake its way through the tubing. It had just a few more inches. There were things he wanted to say, but he figured he could use the sleep first – then he could figure out what words to use. "Fine, but... Ife?"

"Yes, chuck?" Ife gave a kind smile and put a hand on his.

"Can you and I have a private one-on-one when I'm up again?"

"Certainly."

The sedative-laced Evermore finally reached the vein on his left hand. He took another deep breath. A second later, his features fell and his muscles relaxed. His eyes closed, and the veins in his face, neck and arms sunk inward, creating an eerie shadowy effect as vampire sleep enveloped him.

"Alright, all done." Kai rose from his desk, stretching as he made his way to the door. Gibson trailed behind, gathering the scattered documents. When Kai opened the door, he startled slightly at the sight of a woman standing just inches from the threshold.

Her sun-bleached hair framed her face in soft waves. The vibrant red dress she wore accentuated her green eyes, which sparkled with mischief. Her smile was broader, more open, as if she'd just stepped out of a party rather than into a dreary office.

"I was just on my way to the house to pick you up," Kai said, recovering quickly. His cheeks flushed slightly at the sight of her.

"I know," she replied with a light laugh, brushing a strand of hair back. "But I chose to surprise you instead. I'm famished."

"Kate Coupland," she added, extending a hand to Gibson. Her voice carried a melodic cadence, entirely different from the authoritative tone Kai and Gibson had encountered a few months prior on the coast.

Gibson raised an eyebrow. "I remember," he said.

"Oh, of course," Kate said, with a small giggle. "Forgive me. These dates lately have just had me taking leave of my senses!"

"I'll lock up," Gibson offered, taking Kai's keys. "You kids go have your night out on the town."

"Thanks, Gibson," Kai said, taking Kate by the arm. "I'll touch base with you tomorrow."

As they walked away, Gibson frowned, his mind replaying the encounter. "Kate Coupland," he murmured to himself. He shook his head and returned to organizing the documents.

Kai began to walk toward the exit leading to the parking garage. "I assume we're taking *your* car tonight then, Kate?"

"You know it," exclaimed Kate, with a toss of her auburn hair and a vivacious laugh. "Nothing like cruising down the interstate with the drop-top down!"

8
AURORA VULGARIS

Hunter awoke 26 hours later, tears streaming down his face. They had started shortly after he was sedated, and hadn't stopped since. The pillow and the clinical sheets underneath his head were soaking wet.

"Dear Hunter." Ife's brogue was soft and almost motherly as she dabbed a tissue under each of his eyes.

"It won't stop," Hunter shuddered.

"What won't?"

"The dreams," he said. "It won't give me a moment's peace. Every minute I was asleep, it was beside me."

Ife's brows furrowed. "What was beside you?"

"I..." Hunter closed his eyes and shook his head. "I couldn't possibly begin to explain it."

Ife decided to try a bit of reverse psychology. "Oh. Alright. I thought perhaps you trusted me enough that you could tell me anything."

"It's not that." Hunter pushed himself up into a sitting position on the gurney. "It's just something that I know isn't normal – even for all *this*." He gestured at his body and the room surrounding them.

Ife nodded in understanding. Looking first at the floor, she considered her words before looking at Hunter directly in the eyes and asked, "Do you think you could *show* me?"

Hunter tensed immediately at the notion. "I don't want to hurt you," he said.

It was a valid concern. In a practice first observed only within him, Hunter had the capability of projecting mental pictures into the ether, so that people within his proximity could see. Beyond that, if he tapped into vivid memories – his own or that of someone whose mind he was reading – that were tied to particular feelings or sensations, he could make people feel those feelings and sensations in real life. Wounds that were inflicted in the past could appear on the bodies of anyone within his field of vision if he wanted.

"You won't hurt me if you focus on projecting only the images," Ife replied. "Mind over matter."

Hunter's face was a picture of apprehension.

"Trust me," Ife said. "I trust *you*."

Slicer and Kate sat at one end of the room - a disused lecture hall, installed deep within this strange Alaskan cavern repurposed by The Order. At the opposite end of the room, Hunter and Ife sat in roller chairs on a dais perforated by a metallic railing where the lecturer would stand. With Ife and Hunter's serious expressions in this setting, Slicer was reminded of the game show where in the final round, the player and the celebrity guest sat in much the same position, prepared to read off a list of six mystery clues for the player to guess.

"Since you two have never witnessed this personally before," Ife said, "I figured this would be a good learning opportunity. We call the ability we're about to demonstrate 'Mind's Eye.'

"Put simply, it's an extension of the vampire's natural ability to influence a human's thoughts and behaviors – but in a much more... *immersive* way." Ife nodded at Hunter. "Ready when you are."

"Slicer?" Hunter looked at him. "If it any point it looks like Dr. Ife is in any *real* danger – rein me in." Still shirtless, he tapped the tattoo with his right palm.

"You got it, pup," Slicer said, completely unsure of what Hunter truly meant. He and Kate exchanged confused glances.

"What do you want me to show you?"

Ife pondered briefly. "Take me through the worst part of the last dream," she responded. "Or, if that's too painful for you, maybe show me the parts that are most repetitive. You said this is a nightly occurrence?"

Hunter's head dipped slightly. "Every night for the last few months," he said. "It's always different... with just one exception."

"Show me."

Hunter gulped and gripped the sides of his chair. Steeling himself, he relaxed his facial features and looked deep into the eyes of the woman seated across from him. Two pinpoints of bright purple light began to form in his irises. Then, in a twirling motion, the light filled his eyes entirely. Slicer and Kate watched as Ife's eyes began to mirror Hunter's, filling with the same magical light.

Slicer noticed a thin black film materializing above Hunter and Ife, stretching into a shimmering dome that sealed them off from the room. From inside, it was absolute blackness—an empty void waiting to be filled.

Hunter could project any scene he could imagine. He began to piece together that scene like pieces of a torn magazine page being reassembled.

Within seconds, the void transformed into a dim, medieval dungeon. The rough stone walls glistened with dampness, and torches cast flickering shadows. Behind Ife, two platforms bore the shriveled, bound forms of Gibson and Kai, their gray skin stretched taut over lifeless bones. Their legs were shackled and pinned to the rough, splintery wooden planks. Chains stretched taut from Hunter to the bound figures, their metallic clinking echoing ominously. Each movement sent a jolt of agony through the dungeon, Gibson and Kai's cries reverberating as if the air itself recoiled.

"I can't bear to move," Hunter said, his voice feeble and withered. Bold, blood-red tears streamed from the corners of his eyes, which were filled with a purple glow.

"What happens if you do?" Ife's voice was serious but still calming.

To demonstrate, Hunter lifted his right arm so it crossed his chest. The chain connected to that arm pulled taut. Though Ife was not facing them, she could hear the agonized cries of Kai and Gibson and knew that the chain was pulling at their tortured arms. She could hear bones cracking as they were pulled from sockets.

"If I try to relax my arm..." Hunter murmured, and he did so. The cries only intensified. "No matter what I try to do, no matter what moves I make..."

He grimaced for what was to come. He rested both arms defeatedly at the sides of his chair and watched as what always happened next played out. The chains drew themselves even closer in Hunter's direction, and the pallid, corpse-like bodies of his two lovers broke like wafer cookies being snapped in twain. Black, oil-like fluid spurted from the bisected bodies as the top halves crashed to the floor, and pieces of the lower halves spilled out over the platform like cubes of beef being slid off a chopping block.

The chains continued to retract, pulling the torsos of the two vampires ever closer to Hunter, and now into Ife's eyeline. His eyes still blazed a brilliant violet as he continued to project his dream into this grotesque amphitheater.

Slicer turned again to look at Kate. She was leaned forward in her chair, her eyes wide as if she were a four-year-old girl being taken to the zoo for the very first time. She stared agape at the scene playing out before her. "Fascinating," she breathed, her voice barely audible.

Slicer frowned, his stubble causing deep lines around his mouth and chin. His nose twitched.

"This is what he does, Doctor." The voice coming from Hunter's mouth was not his own. Ife twitched. "He tortures *himself* each night with these images. These dreamscapes are his own affair. That's not my doing. My business is with the past."

The purple light suddenly died from Hunter's eyes, and his head slumped forward lifelessly.

"H-Hunter?" Ife's voice quivered. "Are you alright?"

As the dungeon dissolved, a smoky figure emerged behind Hunter, its ember-red eyes glowing like coals. "He relives this every night," it purred, the air thick with its acrid presence. "And I ensure he never forgets.

"Hunter deludes himself into thinking these are scenes from some distant future," the figure explained. It had developed ember-red beads for eyes and gleaming white teeth as it spoke. "Silly boy. He knows he doesn't *have* a future. It's my job to remind him *why*. Allow me to demonstrate..."

The wisps of smoke trailing from the figure, like arms and hands, gestured as the gray canvas flickered to life. The dome surrounding them now acted as a 360-degree slideshow. Ife was a helpless captive, seeing figments of Hunter's memories, and in some cases, imagined pictures as if from a third-party camera, of various moments of trauma from his life...

Falling from a shopping cart at the age of three and cracking his skull on the floor – complete with the X-ray showing the fragment of bone that had threatened to sever an artery...

Riding in the car with his mother... rather, the woman who'd always *claimed* was his mother... who orders Hunter to the floorboard. The four-year-old Hunter is staring through the rear window of the car at a tornado landing on the highway just behind them...

Which led him to remember the incident several months back, also in a car, when he tried to protect his friend and fellow agent Albert when a harpoon gun was fired at them. He had only succeeded in getting them both pierced by the arrow-like blades. He could still feel the harpoon stab through him. Ife held her hands against her chest, feeling the same sensation Hunter was feeling, coupled by the intense cold feeling Hunter remembered later at a hospital when he learned Albert had not survived the attack.

Of course, being pierced in the gut was something Hunter had experienced previously. The moment a chef's knife was plunged into him back at the InnerCore offices in Dallas again filled his memory – and Ife's eyes.

That was followed by a series of tableaux and mental photographs, each capturing in artistic and glossy detail every major event of extreme sadness and pain in Hunter's life.

"These take just milliseconds," the ghostly visage leered. Ife watched as it knelt down beside Hunter's slumped body. A cloud of black smoke shaped like a tongue snaked from the head of the figure and caressed Hunter's right ear lobe, seeming to lick at him as it smirked. "But to Hunter, he relives these memories from beginning to end, moment by moment, second by agonizing second. A constant reminder of what a *failure* he is. And a personal reminder, from me to him, of what he can do to stop it. If done correctly, that is."

More mental Kodaks flashed around them...

Age 30. The razor blade in the Electric Six bathroom, and the interruption from a ruckus outside...

Age 26. His uncle's Winchester shotgun, so conveniently left in the unlocked cabinet next to the opened box of shells... Ife could feel Hunter's sense of touch when he took it off the rack – then a sudden flash as that sensation changed to the feeling of cold gunmetal underneath his chin... then another flash as the gun was unloaded, the shells put back in their box, the gun back on the rack, and the door closed...

Age 9. The garden hose in his grandmother's shed, hung over the wire-basket style light fixture... And the crash of his body to the floor when the fixture wouldn't support his weight when he tried to jump from a stack of boxes.

Nine? Ife thought to herself with a sense of shock. *The dear soul...*

"So many opportunities, such beautiful ways to go," the specter lamented. "He failed each and every time. Much like he always fails..." The laugh in its wicked voice made Ife's skin crawl. They both knew Hunter, even in his suspended state, could hear their conversation. "The splatter from the shotgun would have been *particularly* artistic. But nothing I can't rectify in due course."

"Are you unaware of the fact that he's immortal now?" Her jaw set as she spoke.

"A mere trifle, girl." The smoke monster slid its way around to stare Ife down, face-to-face. "Only *I* can reach him where it truly matters. Only *I* can take him back and allow him the chance to finish what he's so often tried to do."

The figure's acrid, oily-black cloud began to fill the dome surrounding them.

"And believe me," it growled. "I *will* win out."

The smoke dissipated.

Hunter's body slumped forward further and fell out of the chair entirely. The shock of contact with the floor broke the trance, and the dome around them blinked out of existence.

Slicer hurried out of his seat and rushed to Hunter's side. Ife was already gently brushing his hair back.

Hunter's eyes were pooled with red, bloody tears. "I thought this would stop when I was turned," he said, his voice cracking and weak. "I truly did. Why won't it stop?"

Ife sat on the floor next to Hunter. She scooped him up and held him tightly. Looking up at Slicer, she whispered. "Give us the room, please?"

Slicer hesitated, his face a measure of stunned concern. But he eventually nodded and turned toward the exit. He stopped beside Kate's chair. She was still staring out at Ife and Hunter with a thoughtful and thoroughly engrossed expression. He snapped his fingers in front of her face and motioned for her to leave behind him.

Hunter's shuddering began to slow, his head resting against her shoulder. "Why won't it stop?" he whispered, his voice hoarse.

"I don't know yet," Ife admitted, her eyes distant for a moment before focusing on him. "But I promise, Hunter. We'll make it stop."

He closed his eyes, her steady embrace the first comfort he'd felt in what seemed like ages.

Gibson's finger hovered over the call button, his jaw tightening at the sight of the contact name: Hunter II.

He'd spent hours staring at it, each attempt thwarted by a sharp tug of disgust—a craving for violence.

Why not cross realms, confront the bastard, and sever his head from his spine?

Because of his damned oath to be good, he reminded himself bitterly, locking the screen again. One slip, and his tenuous standing with The Order would collapse—along with his existence.

He took a moment or two to collect his thoughts, then reached for the phone again. He selected the contact for Noah Frank and initiated the call.

"Agent Frank," Noah said on the other end of the line.

"Agent Gibson here," Gibson said. "How's life on the other plane of existence?"

"Oh, you know." Noah's response was flat – unusual, for what little interaction Gibson remembered of him. "Is there something I can do for you?"

"Yes, possibly." Absently thumbing through the documents laid out on the desk before him, Gibson cleared his throat, wanting to make sure he didn't come off glib when he spoke. "I'm calling on behalf of Kai. He and I are working on a case and could use some guidance on matters that might involve your new territory."

"How so?"

"Uh, demon saliva," Gibson said. "And venom. Trafficking of such substances across the astral plane and between our two dimensions – could we schedule some time to discuss it?"

"Sure," Noah said. His tone was polite, yet couldn't quite hide a sense of displeasure in his response. "What time is it over there?"

"It's 3 a.m. here," Gibson replied.

"Still adjusting to the differences," Noah said. "Days are longer here, thanks to something they call *aurora vulgaris.*"

"Makes sense," Gibson said flatly.

Gibson could hear the clacking of computer keys from Noah's end. "How about first thing after nightfall your time tomorrow? It should be near the end of my shift today."

Gibson knew that sentence made more sense to Noah than it would to him. "Sure. I know Kai will be eager to see you and curious to see what you've done with the building The Order obtained for you."

"How've you three been?"

The question landed like a punch. Gibson hesitated, his throat tight. "Trucking along," he managed. "Hunter's... working on himself in Alaska. Kai's, uh, exploring his options."

"Dating?" Noah sounded genuinely surprised. "Didn't expect that."

"Me neither," Gibson muttered. "But it's his choice."

"Indeed."

Another awkward pause.

"We'll see you tomorrow, then?" Noah asked, his tone polite but distant.

"Sure," Gibson said, ending the call with a tap.

He set the phone down and leaned back in his chair, running a hand through his hair. His conversation with Noah left an unease gnawing at him—a reminder of how fragile their connections had become. Kai's recent detachment, Hunter's struggles, his own unresolved anger... they all felt like threads pulling taut, threatening to snap.

He reached for the bottle of pre-drawn blood on his desk, staring through it at the faint, flickering shadows on the far wall. He'd never felt more uncertain about the path ahead.

His phone buzzed, snapping him out of his thoughts. He glanced at the screen, frowning as he saw the name.

"Gibson." The voice on the other end sounded like Hunter, only the slightest bit deeper.

"What do you want?" Gibson spoke to the alternate-reality Hunter like the annoyance Gibson considered him.

"I've been receiving the sensations Hunter... *your* Hunter has been sending out – he's having breakouts, isn't he?" This Hunter sounded dead serious.

"Yes," Gibson replied. "We sent him to a safe location so he can go through the motions of the ice-and-fire eruptions."

The other-world Hunter at the end of the line sighed. "That's the last thing he needs right now," he said. "Who's with him?"

"What business is it of yours?"

"Gibson!" The deeper-voiced Hunter's edge took Gibson by surprise. "I'm not playing games here. He could be in *serious danger*. Who is with him?"

"Three of our agents are up in Alaska keeping watch over him - what's this about danger?"

"He has much more than demonic puberty to deal with – he's got borderline personality disorder. If he's in a severe depressive episode while he's going through the extreme hot and cold thing, he could become suicidal. And if he's not watched over *every minute*, he could go through with it."

Gibson's heart lurched. A rush of guilt and dread swallowed him whole, leaving just one fragile thought clawing its way out.

"He... he never told me."

"For how long has this gone on?" Ife asked.

She and Hunter sat on the floor of the lecture hall, the LED lights hanging above the dais the only ones left on.

"I was diagnosed as clinically depressed when I was ten," Hunter said, his voice tired and ragged. "Shortly after I tried to hang myself in the shed. My grandma, she – she went into a major case of denial when the psychiatrist told her, and she never took me to an appointment again.

"She helped me move into the dorms my first day of college," he continued. "On the second day of college I went to the student health center and got started on Wellbutrin. A few years later, the diagnosis changed to borderline personality disorder and the medications and therapy sessions changed."

Ife put her hands behind her head and she closed her eyes thoughtfully. "And I suppose that stopped when you joined up with The Order?"

"By necessity, I figured I'd have to stop seeing my usual doc, yeah," Hunter said. He drew absently on the floor with a finger. "And then, when Kai turned me..."

"You figured having your *human* life ended would end the suicidal thoughts," Ife said. She smiled kindly. "It makes perfect sense. You reckoned that vampirism would be a way to screw over the depression. I get it."

"But I was wrong," Hunter said.

"I know, it's a tough pill to swallow. But that's how it works, kid." Ife sighed and hoisted herself off the floor, then held out a hand to help Hunter to his feet. "I remember you complaining once that you were disappointed your body didn't turn into a 100% physically fit specimen when you became vampire."

Hunter nodded.

"Your brain's sharper, sure, but it's still wired the same way it was before you turned," Ife said.

Hunter rolled his eyes. "I've gathered that, thanks." He scowled. Then he and Ife caught each other's glances, and they shared a gentle laugh.

"So," Hunter sighed. "I guess therapy and medication will have to continue."

"Yep," Ife said. They began to walk up the aisle toward the exit doors.

Hunter's gaze dropped to the floor as they moved. Therapy and medication. It felt like a ball and chain he couldn't shake—a permanent tether to a part of himself he hated. He wanted to believe that his transformation had freed him, that he could be stronger, better. But the truth was glaringly obvious: vampirism didn't cure a broken mind.

The thought gnawed at him until he spoke aloud, his voice low. "I hate that I can't just... fix this." He glanced at Ife, who watched him with steady patience. "But if it keeps me alive, so to speak—keeps me from that ledge—I guess it's worth it."

Ife gave him a warm smile and patted his shoulder. "You're damn right it is. I'll get you set up with the necessary appointments as soon as we get outta this ice cube of a state."

"What do I do in the meantime?" Hunter scratched the back of his head. "While I'm doing this Human Torch-versus-Iceman thing? 'Cause I know it's not helping me."

"No, definitely not." Ife muttered to herself for a moment. "This Slicer fella," she said. "It seems as if you trust him?"

"Totally," Hunter replied.

"Good. I'll have a word with him and come up with a game plan. What about Miss Coupland?"

Hunter shrugged. "I've only met her in passing a few times," he said. "I certainly don't know her well enough."

"Fine," Ife said with a reassuring smile. "We'll work with what we've got."

There was a gurgling noise coming from Hunter's midsection. "Hungry?" Ife asked.

Hunter shook his head no. "I think I'm about to have another flamethrower session," he grimaced.

"Let's get you back outside then."

Following Ife out into the hall and toward the snowy outcrop waiting beyond the steel doors, Hunter thought about how he had believed, incorrectly, that he'd left his troubled past life behind him, and how that continued imbalance in his mind was sending him into a cyclone of confused emotions.

He had to win this fight, he told himself, as the steel doors loomed ahead and the icy wind beckoned. He couldn't afford to lose—not to himself, not now.

9
TAILSPIN

The evening following his banishment, Caeden awoke in the hastily dug sleeping hole he had made for himself. He lay motionless, unwilling to climb out, the weight of grief pressing him into the cold earth. He wished he were truly dead. It felt as though he had lost a loved one –and in a way, he had. He had assumed that the feelings he and Spencer were exploring were those of love, and that love had been snatched away before it could fully bloom.

What if William was right? The thought sank its claws into him. *What if everything I felt for Spencer was tainted? What if the rogue blood made me this way–broken, unnatural, disgusting?*

The question cycled through his mind, looping endlessly until it scraped raw. Eventually, Caeden forced himself to move, clawing his way out of the hovel. The moment he surfaced, he winced at the tearing sound of fabric. A branch or root had snagged his sleeve, but he didn't bother inspecting the damage. The clothes were ruined anyway–Olivia's gift, torn and ragged from his restless burrowing.

Caeden stumbled aimlessly into the woods, brambles clawing at his legs and thorns pricking his skin. He didn't care. His thoughts swirled, heavy and inescapable. He felt as if he were standing on the edge of a vast precipice, teetering with no safety net. The smallest gust of wind might send him spiraling into oblivion.

He walked and walked, the forest closing in around him, his mind a torrent of sorrow. And then, through the dim light of the trees, he saw it again–the cloaked figure.

A few hundred feet away, the figure stood, its outline sharp against the darkness. It seemed to be writing something on paper or slate. The moment it noticed him watching, it vanished into the shadows.

Caeden's chest tightened, anger rising like bile in his throat. "What do you want from me?!" he screamed, his voice echoing through the trees.

Storming toward where the figure had been, he failed to notice the snake crossing his path until its fangs sank into his ankle.

"Owwww!"

He recoiled, stumbling to the ground. The bite marks on his leg sealed almost immediately, but not before the venom began to course through him. A sharp, buzzing heat surged through his veins, like the sickening burn of alcohol–but worse. Much worse.

The venom latched onto the fury already bubbling inside him, twisting it into something darker. Caeden's breathing quickened, his chest heaving as every nerve lit up like fire.

Fight it? a voice whispered in his mind, dark and mocking. *Not a chance in hell.*

"God damn it all!" Caeden roared, his voice shaking the trees. The snake was still slithering away, oblivious to the fury it had ignited. With a growl, he lunged forward, grabbing it by the tail. A savage whip of his arm sent its body smashing against a tree, the impact obliterating it.

The voice in his head was pleased. *More. More death.*

Caeden's vision flooded with red, a fiery aura consuming everything. He didn't just feel power—he *was* power, the kind that demanded submission, the kind that gave him the right to do whatever he wanted.

Panting, trembling with rage, he surged to his feet and began to run. Trees blurred past him, branches snapping underfoot. In his periphery, woodland creatures fled in terror.

Run, you foolish things. Run from Death.

He didn't know where he was going. He didn't care. He only wanted to find something—or someone—to destroy.

And then he sensed it.

A heartbeat.

Tilting his head, he spotted the faint outline of a figure. Was it the cloaked one again? Caeden bared his fangs, his glowing red eyes narrowing. He sprinted toward it, each step faster than the last.

But just as quickly as it had appeared, the figure vanished. Caeden skidded to a halt, growling in frustration. He resumed running, his body a blur of motion as he vaulted over fallen trees and crashed through brush.

Suddenly, the forest gave way to open land. A chill wind swept over him as he stood at the apex of a hill. Below, a vast plain stretched out, dotted with wheat fields, cornfields, and empty farmland. Far in the distance, a tiny farmhouse stood, a plume of smoke curling from its chimney.

Caeden's lips curled into an inhuman smile. Someone was home.

He sprinted down the hill, the farmhouse growing closer with every stride. But as he ran, a new voice–his own voice–shouted from the back of his mind.

Stop it. This isn't right. This isn't you.

The memory of Spencer flickered to life: his smile, the warmth in his voice, the way he had said he cared.

Think of Spencer, the voice begged. *He wants to help. He might even love you.*

But the darker voice drowned it out. *Spencer is off-limits. William made sure of that. They deserve to suffer, all of them.*

The rage consumed him, his vision narrowing as the farmhouse loomed ahead. The door, slightly ajar, swung gently in the breeze.

Open enough, the dark voice hissed. *An invitation.*

Caeden barreled through the door with full force, splinters exploding in every direction. Through the red haze, he caught a glimpse of an elderly man's terrified face.

And then–

Darkness.

Several hours later, Caeden awoke on the cold wooden floor of the farmhouse. For a moment, his surroundings were a blur. The first thing he recognized was the faint orange glow of embers in the fireplace. Without thinking, he rose, grabbed the poker, and stoked the dying fire back to life.

As the flames brightened, his hands caught his attention. They were coated in dried blood, cracked and caked into every crevice. A wave of dread swept over him as fragmented memories from the night before surfaced: the rush of adrenaline, the old man's terrified face, the sound of shattering wood as he burst into the house.

His stomach turned.

Glancing at the mantle, Caeden saw a small oil lamp and a box of matches. His hands trembled as he struck a match, lit the lamp's wick, and turned to survey the room. The light revealed a nightmarish scene. The floor was soaked in blood, a grotesque mosaic stretching corner to corner. Walls and cabinets were smeared with crimson splatters and blackened clumps of matter.

A shudder coursed through him as his foot slipped on something soft and slick. He lowered the lamp, his heart pounding. There, at his feet, lay a mound of flesh and bone, piled like refuse.

"No," he whispered, shaking his head. "No, this isn't..."

He knelt, desperate to convince himself it was a hallucination. Reaching into the pile, his fingers brushed against something solid. He lifted it slowly, his breath hitching. It was the old man's spinal column, its jagged edges protruding from the gore. Caeden recoiled, his hands trembling. He turned his gaze to the far corner of the room, where the man's severed head rested against the wall, its glassy eyes wide, its mouth frozen in an eternal scream.

Caeden retched, collapsing onto his hands and knees. The room spun around him as guilt and horror clawed at his mind. This can't be real. This can't be me.

A sudden misstep sent him stumbling toward the kitchen. The oil lamp slipped from his grasp, shattering against a chair. Flames erupted, greedily devouring the spilled oil and spreading across the blood-soaked floor.

Panic seized him. The fire surged, licking at the walls and swallowing the house in an instant. Caeden had no choice but to dive through the gaping hole where the door had once stood. He hit the ground hard and scrambled to his feet, the roaring inferno behind him lighting up the night.

He ran. His legs carried him blindly into the forest, tears streaming down his face. But these weren't ordinary tears. Blood, fresh and warm, trickled from his eyes, staining his cheeks. He didn't stop until he reached a massive tree, its ancient roots anchoring it like a sentinel. Throwing himself against its trunk, he clung to it, sobbing into the rough bark.

"I'm not a monster," he cried, his voice muffled. "I swear, I'm not a monster! I'm not..."

"I know you're not," came a calm voice behind him. "But... sadly... you can't stop yourself from acting like one."

Caeden spun around to find Olivia standing a few yards away, a satchel slung over her shoulder. Her face was stern but tinged with sorrow. He crumpled to the ground, his sobs renewed.

"I'm sorry," he whispered, rocking back and forth. "I'm so sorry..."

"I know," Olivia said softly. She approached, placing a hand on his head. "I know."

Caeden forced himself to speak through his tears. "How did you find me?"

"When you lost control, you sent out a pulse of energy," she explained. "We all felt it. It scared us."

"Even William?"

"Especially William," Olivia said with a faint sigh. "He wanted me to find you and... put an end to this." Caeden flinched as he realized what she meant. "But I won't," she added firmly, pulling a handkerchief from her pocket to wipe the blood from his face.

"What you did with Spencer has nothing to do with being a rogue," she continued. "It's just not something we talk about. But your rage? That's different. You have to learn to control it."

She knelt beside him and gestured to the satchel. "Come. Let's get you cleaned up."

At the river, Caeden scrubbed the blood from his skin, the icy water biting at his flesh. Olivia laid out fresh clothes for him, watching silently as he dressed.

"Does this mean you can convince William to change his mind?" Caeden asked hopefully. "Am I coming back?"

Olivia shook her head. "No, my dear. You've reached a point where it's too dangerous for you to stay. Your rages put all of us at risk–even Spencer."

A single tear slipped down her cheek. "I must ask you to leave by dawn."

Caeden's chest tightened, but he nodded. "Where will I go?"

"That's up to you," Olivia said, handing him the satchel. "Spencer and I packed this. It has tools and supplies. I'll take you to the train depot in Evansville. From there, the world is yours."

At the station, Olivia handed him fifty dollars and removed a ring from her finger. "Keep this with you," she said. "When you feel yourself losing control, hold it tightly. Remember your humanity."

Caeden slipped the ring onto his finger. "Thank you," he said, his voice trembling. "For everything."

"Take care of yourself, Caeden," Olivia replied.

As the train pulled away, Caeden sat among the crates, watching the station fade into the night. He touched the ring, the metal cool against his skin.

"Goodbye, Spencer," he whispered. "I'll never forget you."

10
POLAR VORTEX

"This tea is lovely."

Gibson, dapperly dressed in a sleek, black pinstripe suit, blended in nicely with the rest of the ultra-modern decor of Noah's office. He, Noah, and Kai were seated in blue fabric wingback chairs surrounding a smoked glass coffee table. Kai was struggling to look comfortable. His normally professional-looking attire was wrinkled and spotted with gray balls of lint.

"It is, quite. The one thing I'll never stop being amazed at in this realm is being able to digest human food and drink once again," Noah laughed. "For the first few weeks it was hard to stop overindulging, but after decades of just the taste of blood you really appreciate the nuances of everyday food and drink!"

Gibson delicately swirled a silver spoon in his teacup then drew it across the rim. "The honey is very vibrant, almost spicy."

"As I understand it, the bees from this particular brand pollinate a flower akin to orange blossoms," Noah said. "I'm reading up on the horticulture in this region, and it's very close to our own, except the summer season is shorter so this is a rarer, more expensive type of honey than what you'd find back home."

"Could we please get back to the subject at hand?" Kai's voice was agitated, nervous. "The demon venom, or the saliva."

"One in the same, I'm guessing from the reports the labs have been sending me," Noah said, handing each of them a few sheets of paper. "Enzymes and chemical analysis that are present in samples show the same type of makeup we find in human saliva... along with high amount of a substance much like a narcotic."

"Drugs?" Gibson arched an eyebrow.

"It's closely related to a psychotropic drug," Noah said, tenting his fingertips as he spoke. "It's got chemical properties unseen in modern medical journals."

"That explains why these vials were found along with drug shipments," Kai observed. "Because they *are* drugs. Drugs that won't show up in testing."

"I think it would be safe to assume the traffickers are letting customers know they've got a brand-new thing to try," Noah said.

Gibson had a furtive look on his face. "The whole point of demons producing venom is to track prey," he said. "Whoever's getting this venom has to know that."

"Especially if they're producing it themselves," Kai replied.

"That's a theory that needs more detective work." Noah cleared his throat as he leaned forward in his chair. "Kai, back when we were first learning about these two dimensions, you had been infected with the venom, correct?"

"A *type* of venom, yes." Kai thought back to the night he, Gibson and Hunter were ambushed in a parking garage. Two hitmen – they assumed Crown operatives, because who else would it have been? – managed to shoot Kai and Hunter several times before Hunter could teleport themselves out of harm's way. Hunter, at that point still acclimating to his newfound ability to teleport, accidentally sent Kai to this version of reality, what they eventually called simply 'the Other Realm,' for the first time.

Kai recalled feeling very nauseous – similar to being acutely sea or airsick – and when he went into a restaurant men's room to look himself over, he found the bullets he'd been wounded by exiting his chest and spilling into the sink. On its own merits, it was not unusual, for a vampire's natural ability to repair itself meant foreign bodies would be expelled from the flesh. But the projectiles were covered in a thin film of golden-hued liquid – the demon venom, he later learned. "So it *was* the venom that made me sick after all," Kai noted. "Not the unexpected interdimensional travel."

"For vampire physiology, that seems to be the case," Noah replied. "Initially nausea, then vomiting at the peak of the infection before the symptoms fade away."

Gibson set his teacup down. "We've learned enough since then that the golden hue of that venom is from a specific kind of demon – a *siphonic* demon."

"And that's not the same type we've been finding in Texas." Kai motioned to the various files spread among them. "It's been a blue, sort of purple kind of color. So it's likely the venom being circulated in the narcotic circuits is from a different type of demon."

"Dr. Mugan and our folks back home only know as much as I can teach them about demonology," Gibson said. "And that's based on what I know about demonology from *our* realm. I'm afraid I have never seen venom with these kinds of properties before. So I don't know what kind of demon we may be searching for."

"Luckily," Noah said, with a moment's hesitation, "I know of someone who can help us out on that front."

The sound of the room's door opening interrupted the momentary silence. Then a husky voice cut through the air.

"Hey, Noah. I needed to come in early to get my – oh!"

Noah bit his lower lip.

Gibson and Kai turned their heads in the direction of the voice. A stocky, redheaded man smiled bashfully at the assembled group.

"I'm so sorry; I didn't realize you had guests."

Noah's voice wavered a bit. "It's quite alright. Gibson? Kai? I'd like for you to meet... my partner. Al."

"Al." Kai repeated the name flatly. He remembered the name. And the face. Gibson recognized the face, but unlike Kai, his expression was one of genuine surprise.

They were all looking at the dead ringer of Albert, Noah's former lover from the other realm.

Noah's *dead* lover from the other realm.

"There are about thirty of us in the pack," Slicer said nonchalantly as he blew on a paper cup full of hot, barely flavorful coffee. "That Calhoun guy called us up to transfer from Ward 8 about a year or two ago."

He and Ife were trying to get better acquainted over what would charitably be called 'break room snacks' – bad coffee and even worse sandwiches found rotating for God knows how long in a fluorescent-lit vending machine. The scent of antiseptic and machine oil lingered in the air, a sterile reminder of where they were.

The hum of nearby equipment, running diagnostics on Hunter's body chemistry, seemed to vibrate through the walls, causing Ife, who had asked Slicer about his background to begin with, to lose focus.

"You're quiet," he said, his voice low but rich, tinged with amusement.

Ife didn't immediately respond, but there was a slight shift in her posture. She knew he was watching her. She finally refocused, her tired eyes meeting his, and gave him a weary smile.

"Busy thinking," she replied, wiping her hands on a cloth before placing it on the table. "About the last test results. Hunter's body... he's not handling this well. There's so much going on inside him. It's like his physiology is rebelling against itself."

Slicer let out a low chuckle, though it was tinged with something darker, a hint of disbelief. "What did you expect? He's a walking contradiction. Vampire... demon. I'm amazed he's still standing."

Ife frowned, a line of concern forming between her brows. *If only he knew the full story like I do*, she thought.

"I know, but his body can't be this unstable much longer. His cells can't keep up with the changes."

Before Slicer could respond, the door to the break room opened with a soft whine, and a sharp, authoritative voice cut through the silence.

"I didn't expect to find you two still here."

Kate Coupland entered the room with an air of authority that felt more like a challenge than an invitation. She was dressed in a sleek, dark jacket, her posture rigid, her presence imposing in a way that suggested she was used to being in control.

She took a moment to glance at the both of them—Slicer, leaning back in his chair, looking almost too relaxed for someone in a situation like this, and Ife, who was still holding onto that same thread of concern she'd been carrying since her talk with Hunter.

"You're still here, then," Kate repeated, her voice almost cold as her eyes scanned the pair. "I believe my crew here will have more than enough resources to carry through watching over Hunter at this point. You two can go find your other companion and head back to Texas and California if you wish."

Slicer raised an eyebrow, leaning forward slightly, a lazy smile still playing at the edges of his lips. "You might have other priorities, but we're not going anywhere. Not until Hunter's stable."

Kate's eyes flickered briefly. Then, with an almost imperceptible sigh, she looked at Ife. "Doctor, you're far too dedicated to this. You have other responsibilities waiting for you in San Francisco. *Your* job doesn't end here. Don't you want to go back to what you know? To *real* work?"

Ife frowned, but she didn't immediately respond. Slicer's gaze shifted between them, sensing the tension building. He already knew what Kate was about to do—this wasn't just a request. It was a command.

"You're both out of your depth," Kate continued, her eyes narrowing as she locked onto Ife. "The Order doesn't need you here for whatever *personal* reasons you think you have. This isn't a rescue mission. It's research. And *you*," she gestured at Slicer, her lips twitching into a faint smirk, "might be better off going back to your... barkeeper's duties. We have things under control."

Slicer leaned forward, his tone quiet but carrying an edge. "You *think* you've got things under control."

Kate met his gaze, her lips pressing together into a thin line. "This is bigger than you, Slicer. And it's bigger than your... friend here." She turned her gaze back to Ife, her smile thin. "You should know that. This isn't the time to get attached."

Ife's jaw tightened. "I'm not going anywhere."

For a moment, the room was thick with tension, as if the air itself was holding its breath. Slicer could almost feel the tug-of-war taking place between Kate's calculated words and Ife's growing defiance. He knew where this was heading. But what he couldn't tell was whether Ife would be able to stand her ground against Kate.

Kate didn't break eye contact with either of them. "Very well," she said, her voice now laced with something almost threatening. "But don't say I didn't warn you."

With that, she turned on her heel and walked back out the door, leaving a lingering chill in her wake.

Slicer leaned back in his chair again, letting out a low breath, the tension momentarily dissipating. "That's one way to ruin a good conversation," he muttered, half to himself.

Ife stood still for a moment, trying to process Kate's words. Then, finally, she spoke, her voice steady despite the storm brewing behind her eyes.

"We're not leaving," she said, her words firm.

Slicer gave a small, approving nod. "Good choice, doc. Now, let's figure out what our next steps are with Hunter."

The air in Noah's office shifted with a subtle but undeniable tension, like the weight of unspoken things that neither Kai nor Gibson were prepared to confront. Al stood awkwardly in the doorway, his red hair bright against the muted tones of the office. He wore a faded blue cardigan over a simple t-shirt and dark jeans, an almost too casual contrast to the immaculate setting. His eyes flickered nervously from Noah to the two visitors.

Noah cleared his throat, visibly uncomfortable. "Al, this is Gibson, and Kai," he gestured to each of them in turn. "We've worked together in the past on several... well, complicated cases. These two are my closest allies, in both worlds." He gave a strained smile, his hands pressing together as though to ward off any further awkwardness. "Gibson, Kai, this is Al. Al's been helping me with some of the, uh, more intricate details of local lore and demonology here."

Gibson blinked, then smiled as if he hadn't been caught off guard at all, though his voice was cool when he spoke. "Charmed." He extended his hand to Al, though his eyes never left Noah.

Al hesitated for a moment, his gaze flicking nervously to Noah, but then he took Gibson's hand, shaking it firmly.

Kai leaned back in his chair as he looked Al over. He couldn't quite place it, but the sensation of *deja vu* was almost suffocating. "We've met, actually. At the pharmacy."

Kai had visited a drugstore shortly after he was flung accidentally into this alternate dimension. Al, the store manager, was unable to sell to him because Kai tried to pay with paper currency native to his realm, and not the one he had been transported to.

"So you're the expert we've been hearing about. The demonologist." Kai's voice was measured, but his eyes narrowed as if trying to assess Al's every move.

Al nodded, scratching the back of his neck. "Yeah, I guess you could say that. I've been around long enough to know my way around a few things." He glanced over at Noah, his eyes asking an unspoken question, but quickly turned back to the others. "But I'm guessing you're not here for the 'tourist info' on the local demons, huh?"

Kai's lips curled into a tight smile, a little more biting than friendly. "I suppose not." He set the papers down and folded his arms. "We've encountered something new. Venom, slash saliva, from a type of demon we haven't identified yet in our neck of the woods. It's being trafficked through some narcotic routes."

Al raised an eyebrow, his interest piqued. "Venom, huh? Narcotics? That's a hell of a combination." He nodded thoughtfully. "Alright. I'm listening."

Noah shifted in his chair, his posture tense. "Demons aren't exactly well-known in our home turf, Al. And, well, I don't exactly have all the answers. But I'm hoping you might."

Al studied him for a moment, the corners of his mouth thinning as he sucked in a breath. "I might have a couple of ideas." His gaze drifted over to the papers scattered across the coffee table, and he took a slow step closer, examining the reports with a quiet hum of concentration. His fingers brushed over the chemical analyses, and then he froze. "The way this substance is described here... it's not just psychotropic. It's got a specific compound in it—one I've read about in some older texts. Demons used to use it in rituals. But it wasn't ever meant to be used for anything *good*."

Kai leaned forward, his eyes sharpening on Al. "Rituals? What kind of rituals?"

Al met his gaze. "Demon blood magic. They'd use the venom as a sort of 'connector.' A way to bind someone to the demon or the demon's will. It's not just for tracking prey; it's a control mechanism. Those who ingest it—or get infected with it—become... marked." His voice dropped to a whisper, though it carried a chill. "Controlled."

Gibson frowned, his mind working furiously. "A drug to enslave people, then."

Al nodded grimly. "Exactly. And it's not just anyone who can make this. It's a specialized kind of demon—*Greater Rakhion* is what it's called in my texts. They're rare, and they don't like to be seen. They operate mostly in the shadows, feeding off negative emotions and using their venom to manipulate people."

Gibson raised a finger as if asking permission to speak, though he didn't wait to be called on. "When you say 'negative emotions,' do you mean the everyday things like sadness and disappointment?"

Al sat on the corner of Noah's desk, his back toward Kai. Kai frowned as he stared at Al. This person was almost identical to the deceased Albert in every way, right down to his bad habits and occasional rudeness. He looked at Noah, who was giving him an apologetic smile in return.

Just like he always did with Albert, Kai thought.

Al replied to Gibson, oblivious to Noah and Kai behind him. "No, I'm talking *negative* negative, like dark and depressing, negative emotions."

"Depression?" Gibson's tone sharpened. "Would people with certain emotional disorders be susceptible?"

Al looked at the ceiling thoughtfully. "I suppose so," he said.

Gibson set his cup and saucer on the coffee table and stood. "I need to go," he said.

Surprised, Kai stood as well. "What? Why?"

"I need to go see the other Hunter immediately." Gibson's voice denoted restraint despite a rising panic.

11
CONVERGENCE

The air in Neptunes, a windowless music club with grimy black walls, was thick and oppressive, the kind of atmosphere that clung to the skin like the smell of stale vape clouds. Gibson climbed up the metallic grated steps leading from the front lobby to the loft above, his boots echoing in the emptiness. The dim, flickering light from wall-mounted sconces painted his sharp features in shifting shadows, accentuating the unnatural hue of his eyes —glowing emerald green betraying his underlying worry and concern.

When he opened the door waiting at the top of the steps, his undead heart leapt when he saw Hunter waiting for him on a leather sofa. Then his brain clicked into gear, and he reminded himself that this wasn't his Hunter. Despite looking virtually identical to the vampire-demon he had grown to love and cherish, the man before him now was in no way identical. The man's demeanor was calm, but his eyes betrayed a storm of thoughts as they followed Gibson's approach. He gestured to the empty chair across from him, his fingerless-gloved hand steady.

"Gibson," the alternate-world Hunter greeted, his voice smooth but edged with a weight just slightly deeper than Gibson's betrothed. "I was starting to think you'd never make it."

"This version of Dallas is cumbersome to get around when you're familiar with an entirely different map," Gibson replied, lowering himself into the seat. His tone was curt, but his gaze remained fixed on Hunter II, studying the man as if he were a puzzle missing half its pieces. "I need to know more about you and your bandmate, Devon."

"What would you like to know?"

"Are either of you *Greater Rakhion*?"

Hunter II lifted his eyebrows in surprise. "I didn't know you were familiar with that name."

"Only very briefly," Gibson said. He spouted back the few details Al had taught him an hour or so earlier, and what he'd learned about *Greater Rakhion* demons attracted to negative energy and those with depression.

"Hunter and Kai have both been exposed to *Greater Rakhion* venom," Gibson said. "I need to know if you're the source of it. You or your drummer."

Hunter II leaned back, folding his hands atop the table. "I wouldn't do that. You know about Hunter Prime's... condition," he began, each word measured. "His depression is a symptom of something larger. His demonic side is growing stronger, Gibson. Evolving. And that's dangerous."

Gibson's jaw tightened. "You think I don't know that? I've been watching it happen. He's slipping."

"Precisely why we need to talk," Hunter II said, leaning forward now, his voice dropping into a conspiratorial whisper. "There's something you need to know. Something I've kept from you, Kai, *and* the other Hunter."

Gibson narrowed his eyes. "Spit it out then. I don't have the patience for riddles."

Hunter II exhaled slowly, as if steeling himself. "I'm employed by The Crown as a Watcher."

The word caused Gibson to tense immediately. Gibson's former role in The Crown had always been fluid – he never committed acts of violence on behalf of the organization, but he had been able to use his powers of manipulation and control to influence others' behavior to those ends. In doing so, he had been aware of the presence of Watchers.

Watchers weren't mere spies–they were architects of observation, tasked with embedding themselves into rival organizations and mapping their weaknesses. Their purpose wasn't just to gather intelligence but to find the pressure points that could shatter alliances, disband factions, or turn allies into enemies.

He had been privy to the training of Watchers, which had been grueling, both physically and psychologically. Watchers were taught to think three steps ahead, to anticipate not just the actions of their targets but the ripple effects those actions would have across the larger geopolitical chessboard. They were manipulators of trust, weaving themselves into the fabric of their targets' lives until their eventual betrayal struck like a perfectly timed blade.

Gibson was aware the job required moral compromises, moments of balance between loyalty against survival. Being a Watcher wasn't just a job; it was an identity.

And here, the carbon copy of Hunter was freely admitting to him that he was one of those Watchers.

Hunter II continued, "My task has been to observe and report on The Order's weaknesses surrounding the three of you. Everything about you, Hunter Prime, Kai… all of it goes back to them."

For a moment, the only sound in the room was the faint hum of the fluorescent lights hanging above them. Gibson felt his insides begin to boil with anger. Then, Gibson's voice cut through the silence, low and lethal. "You've been aware of Hunter's existence for as long as you've been alive, haven't you"

"Yes," Hunter II admitted without flinching. "You've been aware of the Gemini theory, have you not?"

Gibson nodded. The working theory of the Two Realms was based on the notion that every humanoid is created in pairs. By whatever cosmic or metaphysical forces that dictated, one is supposed to be born into each realm. The existence of identical twins in either realm is explained away as an anomaly – an error in the process.

"As soon as The Crown was made aware of your Hunter joining The Order, they went in search of me and recruited me to be a Watcher."

Building the timeline out in his head, Gibson asked, "Did you have anything to do with Hugo in San Francisco?" Hugo, once a young man Gibson had under his personal staff as a source of fresh blood, and sometimes intimate recreation, wound up trying to assassinate him and Hunter Prime when they were in San Francisco.

Hunter's doppelgänger blinked twice, processing the name. "In what way do you mean, 'have anything to do with' him?"

Knowing by that response that he *knew* who Hugo was was enough to send Gibson flying at him, fangs extended, his eye color displaced by a furious red. Hunter II grabbed each of Gibson's arms, locking his own fangs into place in reflex. Equally matched in terms of strength, there was a standoff as muscle pushed against muscle.

"I knew *of* Hugo. From the time you had brought him to Dallas when you were living at the Omni Hotel, yes, I knew of him. I knew he was easily malleable. That's all I told The Crown. Whatever happened to him thereafter was not my doing!

"But that's not the whole story. I'm also working for a third party."

Snarling, Gibson released his grip on this version of Hunter. "Talk," he said.

"It's another organization, based here in this realm and unknown to yours. My real mission is to undermine The Crown. Everything I've told them has been carefully curated to mislead and sabotage their plans."

Gibson's claws extended instinctively, his demonic side flaring in response. He thought back to Hugo. Hugo was a... simple boy, to be charitable. It had been a matter of some curiosity that Hugo of all people would wind up being a Crown assassin. And he had been quickly killed in his first attempt at it. Still...

"And I'm supposed to trust you? After you've just admitted to playing all sides?"

"You're not supposed to trust me," Hunter II said sharply, his own tone gaining an edge. "You're supposed to listen. Hunter–*your* Hunter–is vulnerable. If his evolution isn't managed carefully, The Crown will exploit it. And believe me, they already have plans in motion."

Gibson leaned back, forcing himself to rein in his fury. "Why tell me this now? What's your angle?"

"Because you're the only one who can keep him from falling apart," Hunter II said simply. "Kai, love him as he might, bound by vampire blood as they are, Kai is a liability because he does not share the demonic blood bond you have with Hunter. And because if we don't work together, everything–The Order, The Crown, this third agency–it will all come crashing down. The chaos won't just consume us. It will consume the entirety of both realms."

Gibson's crimson eyes bore into Hunter II's for a long, tense moment. Then, he stood, the chair scraping against the floor. "You've put yourself in a dangerous position. If you're lying, I'll make you regret it."

"I'm counting on you to hold me accountable," Hunter II replied, his voice steady but somber. "But for now, we need to focus on Hunter. The clock is ticking, Gibson. Where is he?"

The sky in the alternate dimension had an eerie, perpetual twilight that cast everything in a soft, golden glow and made Kai realize how *off* everything here seemed compared with his home world. Kai wandered through the Westfellow Market, its stalls laden with fruits that appeared similar to the oranges and apples from home, only bigger; shimmering fabrics, and a few items that defied earthly physics.

It wasn't long before he spotted Al. The man looked uncannily like Albert–same crinkly hair, same crooked smile that could charm anyone. But there was something different in his posture, his energy. This wasn't Albert, and Kai had to remind himself of that fact. It was the whole reason Kai decided to stay in the realm until he heard back from Gibson.

Al stood at a stall, inspecting a collection of intricate clockwork devices. He seemed at ease.

"Al," Kai called, his tone neutral but firm.

Al turned, his face lighting up with recognition. "Kai! Didn't expect to see you here. What brings you to the market?"

Kai didn't bother with pleasantries. "We need to talk."

Al's smile faltered slightly, but he nodded. "Alright. Let's find somewhere quieter."

They moved to a secluded alcove away from the market's chaos. Al leaned against the wall, his arms crossed. "What's on your mind?"

Kai didn't mince words. "Noah."

At the mention of the name, Al's posture stiffened. "What about him?"

"I'm sure you know what," Kai said, his tone sharp. "Noah lost Albert. The man he loved more than anything. And now he's found you–a version of Albert who's alive and breathing. Don't you think that's a little... complicated?"

Al sighed, running a hand through his hair. "Complicated? Sure. But it's not like I planned this, Kai. I didn't ask to be anyone's second chance."

"And yet here you are," Kai said, his voice hardening. "Do you realize what this is doing to him? He hasn't let go of Albert. He's using you as a stand-in, a way to avoid dealing with his grief."

Al's jaw tightened. "I care about Noah. And I'm not blind to what you're saying. But it's not that simple. He's... he's different when he's with me. Happier. Isn't that what matters?"

Kai stepped closer, his eyes narrowing. "Happiness built on a lie doesn't last. You're not Albert. You can't *be* Albert. And the longer this goes on, the harder it's going to be for him to face that truth."

Al stared at Kai for a long moment, as if he had something on the tip of his tongue. Then he looked away, his gaze distant. "I... I didn't want to get involved at first. But Noah... he has this way of pulling you in. Making you believe that maybe, just maybe, you can be enough for him."

Kai conceded the point. He, after all, had felt that way about Noah himself, once upon a time. "But you can't," Kai said bluntly. "Not when he's still holding on to a ghost."

"And what do you suggest I do? Walk away? Leave him to spiral deeper into his grief?"

Kai's voice softened, but only slightly. "You need to help him see that the Albert he knew and loved is gone. That he needs to let go, for his own sake. If you care about him as much as you claim, you'll help him heal, not enable him to stay stuck in the past."

Al's eyes met Kai's, and for a moment, the tension between them was palpable. Then Al nodded slowly. "I... I'll think about it."

Kai placed a hand on Al's shoulder, his expression stern but not unkind. "Do more than think. Do what's right–for both of you."

With that, Kai turned and walked away, leaving Al alone in the golden twilight. The market's noise seemed distant now, and Al felt the weight of Kai's words pressing down on him. He cared about Noah deeply, but he couldn't deny the truth in what Kai had said.

Hunter lay restrained on a reinforced medical bed, his chest heaving as he fought against the lingering tremors of his latest outburst. The walls of the chamber still bore the crystalline scars of his ice missile–jagged shards embedded in steel, glinting under the clinical light. Frost coated the floor, a chilling reminder of the uncontrollable power now coursing through him.

Before the ice, there had been fire.

Moments before the eruption, Hunter's entire body had tensed, his skin glowing faintly as veins of molten orange streaked across his arms. Heat radiated from him in waves, causing the temperature in the room to skyrocket. Alarms blared, and medical staff scrambled to activate containment protocols.

Kate Coupland stood nearby, unflinching as she barked orders into her communicator. "He's destabilizing! Get the suppression field active now!" she commanded.

Hunter's eyes snapped open, glowing a fiery red. His voice, guttural and pained, tore through the chaos. "It's... coming... again. I can't stop it!"

Dr. Ife was the first to approach, her voice steady yet tinged with concern. "Hunter, focus on my voice! You've been through worse. You can control this."

Mugan stood beside her, rapidly analyzing Hunter's vitals. "This isn't just a flare-up. His power's adapting, morphing. We're on borrowed time."

Slicer stood beside Kate, leaning casually against a wall in his default humanoid form, and tilted his head. He said nothing, simply observing as Ife and Mugan consulted notes and devices and as Kate ordered staff members about.

"Dr. Ife, Mugan, Slicer–step back. I need this area cleared," she said.

Ife's brows knitted together. "Kate, you can't isolate him now. He trusts me. If he loses control–"

"That's exactly why you'll be safer out of here," Kate interrupted. "I have the sedative prepped. We need to neutralize this before anyone gets hurt."

Reluctantly, Ife exchanged a glance with Mugan, who nodded solemnly. "Fine. But I'll be monitoring from the control room. Don't push him further than he can handle."

Kate's face was unreadable as she gestured for them to leave. Once they were gone, Slicer lingered a moment longer, as if debating whether to trust her. Eventually, he shrugged and exited, leaving Kate alone with Hunter.

She stepped forward cautiously, her breath visible in the freezing air. Her eyes betrayed a hint of urgency. She adjusted the IV drip with practiced efficiency, the translucent tube snaking down to the needle already inserted into Hunter's arm. She lifted a hefty syringe and inserted the tip into the top of the bag. The IV, full of Evermore, bulged as the new additive was added.

"This is the only way," Kate said softly, her voice steady but tinged with an undertone that Hunter couldn't place.

"You don't get it," Hunter rasped, his voice raw from the strain of resisting his own power. "It's not just the… the abilities. It's *me*. This thing inside me, it's alive. It's waiting for me to give up."

Kate hesitated, her hand brushing against a small pin on her lapel. The insignia bore The Order's emblem. She leaned closer, her voice softening. "Hunter, I know more than you assume. You need rest. Let the sedative do its job. We'll figure this out."

Hunter's head lolled to the side, his vision swimming as the IV began to take effect. He squinted at Kate, the edges of her face blurring. For a moment, he thought he saw something off–the faintest shift in her expression, like a mask slipping. But then the darkness came, and he slipped into unconsciousness.

In the dream, he was no longer in the medical lab. He stood in a void—an endless expanse of shadow punctuated by icy mist curling at his feet. Before him loomed a figure, tall and imposing, its form shifting between a faceless silhouette and something disturbingly familiar. Its voice was a low, resonant growl that reverberated through the void.

"You can't fight me forever, Hunter," it said. "I *am* you. I am every doubt, every failure, every time you wished it would all just end."

Hunter clenched his fists, frost gathering at his fingertips. "You're not me. You're just a parasite."

The figure laughed, a cold, hollow sound. "Denial won't save you. You created me, fed me, nurtured me. I'm the only part of you that's honest."

Ice began to crackle and spread under Hunter's feet as his power surged. "Maybe I did create you. But I'm done letting you control me."

The figure lunged, its shadowy form stretching toward him like a tidal wave. Hunter raised his hands, and an icy barrier erupted between them, sharp and jagged. The clash sent shockwaves through the void, but Hunter stood firm.

"I'm not giving up," he growled. "Not to you. Not to anyone."

The figure recoiled, its form flickering. "You think you can win? You can't destroy what you are."

"Maybe not," Hunter said, his voice steady. "But I can choose what I become."

The void began to shift, the shadows receding as Hunter pressed forward, his ice carving a path through the darkness. The figure's form wavered, shrinking under the weight of Hunter's resolve. The once-overpowering presence now seemed small, almost pitiful.

Back in the medical lab, Kate watched Hunter's vitals stabilize on the monitor. She glanced down at the pin on her lapel, her fingers brushing it absently.

"Sleep well, Hunter," she murmured, her voice carrying an almost imperceptible edge. "We'll see just how far you're willing to fight."

12
SOUTHBOUND & DOWN

Caeden spent two months on the rails, hopping from car to car at each station as the cargo inside was unloaded and transferred.

He fed only sparingly – his depression was so strong that he barely wanted to move at night, much less feed. It was this vampiric urge for blood that got him in the mess he was in, after all. The last thing he wanted was to take blood from any other living being.

But he obviously had to at some point. Rats, mostly. One every other day was enough to satiate his basic need. But something, a germ in that last instance of bloodlust, the urge to feed on a human or a larger animal was proving strong.

There was a war going on inside his head, every waking moment. A three-cornered fight, you might say. One side, the rogue, demanding to be satisfied, demanding blood and violence. Another side, the one still clutching the last few shreds of Caeden's humanity, begging him to be rational. Then, there was a third voice, one just as dangerous as the rogue...

Caeden had become quite adept at rearranging the contents of the shipping crates inside his railcar. Even though it ultimately meant some business would have missing or surplus items when their order was ultimately delivered, he needed the close confines of the container to sleep in during the daytime.

It was the closest thing to a coffin: a sturdy wooden crate, planks packed tightly together. Virtually light-tight. Caeden would pack himself in the box to hide through the daylight hours. It would get quite hot inside as the summer days wore on, and Caeden would not get much sleep.

What he *would* get is a recurring thought. A persuasive, seemingly logical thought.

Do you really want an end to this nightmare of an afterlife you find yourself in? It said this repeatedly. *Simply step out of the box. Step into the light. End it all right now – that'll solve the problem in an instant.*

Caeden hadn't witnessed a vampire dying by the light before, but Olivia and William had. During their nighttime story swaps, they had both discussed some unfortunates who had met the sun. Depending on the time of day or the season, the death was either a minute or two of burning, or a nearly-instantaneous explosion of sparks and ash.

As day rolled on after day, and he spent more and more time confined in shipping containers, Caeden seriously considered just opening the lid, opening the door of the railcar, and letting physics do its job. But another thought also occurred to him: If he had truly wanted to kill himself, he'd had ample opportunities during the journey. But morning after morning, he made the conscious effort to find shelter. He took the time to move the cargo out, and seal himself in.

He realized that just by doing that every day, his subconscious was ready and capable of facing whatever was to come. After that, the war of the mind was easy to *fight*. But it hadn't truly gone away – he had yet to *win* the war.

Caeden traversed the eastern seaboard and the midwest by rail, getting used to determining distance, time, and compass position as the trains interconnected. One day in late September, at a maintenance stop in Chattanooga, Caeden decided now was the time to switch to a passenger service.

But where to go?

Union Station was a grand, ornate building, with white marble columns surrounding a circular atrium, its glass and wrought-iron dome matched in size by a green and blue marble circle on the lobby floor. Caeden marveled at the scale and fancy architecture as he approached a notice board near the restrooms.

He scanned the various pieces of handwritten and mimeographed notes on the board. Some advertised odd jobs there in town; others were selling potential travelers on the prospects of oil boomtowns elsewhere in the country.

"OIL!" boomed one such notice. "Derricks being built as far as the eyes can see - seek your fortune in crude - and live bountifully! AUSTIN, TEXAS."

Curious, Caeden next walked to the schedule board. Looking at the clock next to it, he saw it was 10:59 p.m. There was one train going to Austin - scheduled to leave at 11:15. Throwing his knapsack over his shoulder, he bustled to the ticket desk.

"May I help you?" The agent had short black hair and a smartly tailored outfit. He spoke with a timid but polite Southern accent.

"Yes," Caeden said. "Can you tell me if there are any tickets left for the train to Austin?"

"Quite a few, actually," the agent replied, consulting a chart. "Fares are $1.50 for the standard coaches."

Caeden began to reach in his pants pocket for his wallet when the agent continued to speak.

"We also happen to have an executive coach available for this trip – may I be able to interest you in that?"

Caeden paused. "How much?"

"Ten dollars," the agent said. Noticing Caeden wince at the quote, he quickly made his pitch. "It's a private car. You get a personal concierge, a marvelously comfortable bed, and a full-size bathtub in your quarters."

Caeden hedged. That did sound amazing compared to the stark surroundings he'd been used to on the rails up til now. He wavered. "Ten dollars though, that's a fortune," he mumbled to himself. He had fifty, but who knows how long he'd have to live off it, now that he was venturing into the land of the living.

"You also get private dining privileges," the agent said. He was really eager to make the sale. "Oh, and the windows to your car have velveteen curtains. They do wonders to block out the sun during sunrise and sunset."

Caeden's ears perked. "Sold," he said.

Pleased, the agent got the ticket prepared as Caeden laid the cash on the counter. "Do you require a bellhop to assist with your bags, sir?"

"Ah, no, I just have this," Caeden said, gesturing to his knapsack.

"Very good," said the agent, handing Caeden his ticket. "Platform 3 – and hurry," he said with a courteous smile.

Caeden nodded, thanked the agent, and hurried for the entrance to the train platforms. So enthralled was he with the prospect of boarding a train with a bathtub, to say nothing about the bed, Caeden did not see that the agent, after placing the fare money in the cash drawer, looked out across the lobby and raised his hand, snapped his fingers twice, and nodded.

Nor did Caeden see that the person the agent signaled to, a man wearing a long black coat with a matching hat, and holding a brown folder in his hand, nodded back.

Caeden now had two nights with which to relax and get his thoughts together as he traveled in luxury in the private car.

On the first night, he took advantage of his luxury surroundings by drawing the curtains tight, laying on the plush bed, and falling into a deep sleep. It carried him through the following day, dead to the world.

Caeden's dreams that day were haunted by a repeating series of images, first of the elderly man he slaughtered and eviscerated. He remembered actually sinking his teeth and fangs deep into the flesh, gripping the torso with his fingers, and ripping what he held in his hands far apart with supernatural strength.

He would then remember similar incidents over the last four decades since he was turned – an endless array of memories he thought were dead and buried, come to life fresh once more from his most recent act of carnality. These scenes were also interrupted by the thought of his and Spencer's first and only kiss and how he wanted to *love*... counteracted by what evil *joy* he had felt while letting his rogue side take control.

He remembered the sight of the oil lamp smashing and setting the farmhouse alight, and once the flames that encircled him dissolved into the ether of the dream world, Caeden found himself in a dark, empty void, as alone, cold, and scared as he'd felt so often over the years.

"I won't do it again," he cried out to nobody, as he did so many times when this dream, in its various incarnations, would take hold of him. "I swear to it," he would say, running to every corner of the endless void and finding no egress, no exit. "I swear, I won't kill again!"

The shrill, ear-splitting exclamation of a train whistle jolted Caeden awake from a deep yet unrestful slumber at sundown the next evening.

His eyes passed ornate, gilded-edge furniture and accoutrements; his skin was caressed by the finely-pressed sheets as he laid in the bed, being gently vibrated by the friction of the train car as it idled against the tracks. After a few moments, he got up to gaze out one of the windows. As he looked out over the large swaths of land in his line of sight, his mind hazed over and he thought of Spencer. How lovely it would have been to set up a homestead of their own. A cabin, perhaps, on some farmland here in the plains. Staying in one place, Spencer by his side as they slept cozily...

Oh, Spencer...

There was a quick knock at the door and a bellhop in a crimson-red suit with gold piping poked his head into the cabin. "Pardon me, sir," the young man said politely. "But you have a guest."

"A guest?"

The bellhop gave a single nod and then disappeared behind the door. A split second later another man appeared in the doorway – a man cloaked from head to toe in a black velveteen trench coat and a matching hat that obscured much of his face.

Caeden, blessed or cursed with a superhuman ability to recognize posture and other features from only the briefest of glimpses, immediately connected the visage before him from that of memories from several nights back. This was the person who had been in the forest writing something down. This was the person who Caeden thought had been watching him and Spencer during their clandestine affair.

He also knew it was pointless to confront the man in black with this knowledge. "Who are you?" His demand was terse and edgy. "What do you want of me?"

"First," came the soft-spoken reply, "I wish to assure you that I mean you no harm. Though you and your kindred may not know it, I am well-versed in the history of the vampire, and I am one of a precious few humans in the world that see the advantages of our coexistence."

"That's swell." Caeden's lips remained pursed as he spoke. He clutched the nearest thing to him - his bedsheets - holding them as if they would offer him some degree of protection. "Who are you," he asked again.

Removing his hat, the man revealed a neatly-trimmed head of blonde hair and, in contrast, a stubble that highlighted a somewhat incongruent shape to his face. The man set the hat on the seat of a nearby chair and removed his black leather gloves one finger at a time, before tossing them on top of the hat.

"My name is Sidwell Calhoun," the man said with a slight bow forward. "And *you* are Caeden Taylor. Or, as human records would have you, the *late* Caeden Taylor of Wilmington, North Carolina. Lost in the wreck of the *Monitor* off Cape Hatteras."

Caeden jutted out his jaw. "So you know who I was and what became of me. Why the interest?"

Sidwell pondered his words, staying put just a foot or so beyond the door, which he latched shut behind him. "The organization I work for has begun recording a catalog of vampires," he said. "They have charged me with recruiting potential agents – and with your background they felt you may be an ideal candidate."

"Agents?"

Sidwell nodded. "Forgive the cloak..." and as he said the words, he unhooked a knife, still in its sheath, from his side. He placed the knife alongside the hat and gloves on the chair. "... and the dagger. It is quite necessary. Mine is an organization that demands... order. And with the relatively recent acknowledgment of your kind, there is discord in our ranks.

"Put simply, Mr. Taylor," Sidwell continued, "there is hesitancy about how my organization should view vampires. I have done more research on the subject than anyone in the Northern Hemisphere. I *know* that as a species, you and I can co-exist. We have done for eons. My job is to prove to my superiors that you and your kindred pose no threat to the so-called 'Natural Order.'"

Caeden sighed. "What have you seen of me over the last few days that suggests anything normal?"

"I don't need to answer that," Sidwell said. "I know you've been told about the fate of the rogue, and that any vampire who applies himself can avoid the madness that comes along with it. You have great strength of character – what made you join the crew of the *Monitor* in the first place?"

It was hard for Caeden to think back to the days of the War Between the States, and how he'd lied about his age like so many young men did in order to enlist. "I wanted to fight for what I knew in my heart was right," he said. "I wanted to… to be on the right side of history."

A faint grin developed on Sidwell's thin lips. "Exactly," he said. "That, my boy, is The Order's main purpose – to fight for what's right. You can no longer do that by everyday means. But we could use you. The Order could use you and your convictions. That's why I hired you this rail car, so I could give you a quick history about my organization and how you could help me prove your kind's worth"–

"Just a second," Caeden held up a hand. "*I* paid for this car," he protested.

Sidwell reached into his trouser pocket and pulled out a ten-dollar bank note. "No. I'm afraid the car truly cost more than you had in your possession. I had the ticket agent in Chattanooga give that cock-and-bull story so I could get you on the train." He held the bill out to Caeden.

Incredulous to how fantastical the last few minutes had been, Caeden plucked the money out of Sidwell's fingers.

Sidwell next took out a pocket watch and examined its face. "We have roughly five hours before we pull into the station in Austin. I know I'm asking you to make a tremendous leap of faith, but I think you'll find the work to be just as tremendously rewarding – both financially as well as morally."

Caeden felt a headache developing between his eyes. Knowing the sensation to be a phantom pain, leftover memories of human senses, he ignored it. He gestured to the chair. "I reckon you better take a seat," he said.

"Thank you." Sidwell picked up his accoutrements and sat them in his lap as he took the seat.

"So what is it that…" Caeden began, trailing off almost immediately.

"The Order," Sidwell said, "aims to work to correct the ills of society around the world. Often that entails performing tasks that police cannot or will not do themselves."

"You operate above the law?"

"In the shadow of the law, I suppose you could say." Sidwell shifted the hat on top of the pile of his belongings. "In many instances we are also judge, jury, and executioner for those we find in violation of moral order."

"And you think *I* would work well in this organization?"

"It's a theory," Sidwell said.

"What if I say no?" Caeden folded his arms across his chest.

"You are completely within your rights to do so," Sidwell said. "But you should be aware that I'm going out on quite the limb telling you any of this. Refusal to assist would incur certain repercussions."

Caeden's eyes narrowed. "Is that a threat?"

Sidwell showed a brief glimpse of surprise. "Not at all," he said quickly. "My apologies. I merely meant that I have entrusted you with the knowledge of my group's existence. I would have to swear you to secrecy about that – whether or not you agreed to join us. And there would be an occasional presence by myself, or my eventual successor... *successors*... for as long as you continued to exist. To ensure you didn't spill the beans, so to speak."

"And what is it exactly that you're expecting me to do?"

It was Sidwell's turn to sigh. "There is some... nasty business going on in Texas at present," he said. "Murders. Horrible, grisly deaths. Several women in at least four cities. "We're aware of a connection – the killer is using these very railroads to travel from place to place.

The police in these cities aren't admitting to that because they don't wish to cause a panic in the local press.

"What I am asking you to do," he continued, "is to find out who exactly is committing these crimes, interrogate them, and obtain a confession."

"And then?" Caeden's arms were pressed tighter into his chest.

The grin returned to Sidwell's face. "Then you can unleash your rage upon the miscreant."

Caeden's face opened up in shock. "You what?"

"You feed on blood," Sidwell reasoned. "This person has taken others' lives in the most vicious of ways. The Order would have it that the criminal be dispatched, and you are a natural conduit toward that end. We do the job the police don't want, and in return you satiate your needs and ensure your continued survival."

"You're telling me..." Caeden felt numb as he spoke the words – he couldn't believe he was having this conversation so openly – "I do the job of a police constable, and then, once I obtain a confession... I execute them? Bypassing due process, trial, all that?"

"The legal system, particularly in this part of Texas is... slipshod, at best," Sidwell said. He ran his hand over the brim of his hat as he spoke. "Lynching is still commonplace, even after the War Between the States. If we handle the investigation ourselves, more innocent lives will be saved than if the public learned there was a mad killer among them and people began to make wild and unfounded accusations."

As Sidwell's words hung heavy in the air, Caeden stared at him, the weight of the proposition sinking into his chest like lead. He wasn't entirely unfamiliar with vigilante justice – he'd witnessed it in the death of his maker. But this... this felt different.

The man before him wasn't some simple lawman or an angry mob. He was part of something organized, something that operated in the shadows with purpose and precision. But to do what Sidwell asked of him... to act as detective *and* executioner, to uphold law and order for the masses, yet in a twisted way allowing him to cast off every ounce of humanity he'd fought to hold onto against those found guilty–Caeden's stomach churned at the thought.

"What happens after I do this?" Caeden asked, his voice rougher than he'd intended.

Sidwell's smile never faltered. "You'll be rewarded for your efforts, of course. And we shall rely on your continued services in perpetuity. The Order won't judge you for how you feed, Mr. Taylor. I will see to that. In fact, I believe your kind's very nature could be an asset to the cause. You'll have the freedom to operate as you wish, so long as you deliver results."

Caeden rubbed his eyes, feeling the exhaustion creep up on him once again. The last thing he wanted was to be swept up in some hidden war, to become yet another pawn in someone else's game. But his mind drifted back to those dreams–the carnage, the endless hunger. He felt it again, a gnawing emptiness that only blood could quell.

For a moment, he entertained the idea. Perhaps he could become something more than the broken creature he'd become. Perhaps this Order was the answer. But as quickly as that thought came, it dissolved, leaving behind the same bitter taste that had haunted him for decades.

"I'll think on it," Caeden said, his voice steady despite the turmoil inside. "I need to see Austin first."

Sidwell raised an eyebrow but said nothing. He was clearly a man accustomed to power, to getting what he wanted. But Caeden wasn't so easily swayed.

The train's whistle blew again, a sharp, piercing sound that echoed through the night. Caeden turned his gaze to the window and the plains quickly replaced with farms and, then, homesteads. Austin was quickly approaching. A new place, a new beginning–or perhaps the same cycle continuing, just in a different setting.

"You have until we reach the station to make up your mind," Sidwell said, standing. He replaced his gloves slowly, deliberately, and Caeden noticed how carefully the man adjusted his coat, almost as if he were preparing for something more than just a conversation.

"I'll be ready," Caeden replied, though the uncertainty in his voice betrayed his words.

Sidwell gave him a nod, and with a final glance at the bed and its expensive linens, he turned toward the door. "We'll speak again soon, Mr. Taylor. Remember this, the Order is patient. But we are not idle. And now that you know of its existence, you are a part of our world, one way or another."

As the door clicked shut behind him, Caeden was left alone again in the plush cabin. But for the first time in what felt like years, he didn't immediately feel the need to hide. Instead, he stood and moved to the window, watching as the train pulled into the station.

The simple oil lamplights of Austin's train station stretched out before him, an oasis of promise and danger wrapped in one. A city caught between the Old West and the encroaching modern world.

And Caeden, in the midst of it all, was left to decide: would he stand among the living, tasked with protecting the innocent from the lawless, or simply embrace what he truly was?

A flicker in the back of his head reminded him he also had another option - give up, and await the morning sun.

The train's wheels ground against the tracks, slowing to a stop. He could hear the bustle outside, the footfalls of travelers disembarking, the hiss of steam.

In that brief moment, Caeden Taylor faced his reflection in the glass. He was still haunted by the past, still a man torn between two worlds. But soon, he would have to decide where he would place his allegiance: with the people he once knew, or with the darkness that had become his reality.

The question wasn't whether he could choose.

The question was whether he wanted to.

The doors swung open. The night beckoned.

13
VOLATILE CLIMATES

"I bet you could use some good news right now," Kate's voice carried an overly chipper tone that made Hunter's skin prickle. His first instinct was to tell her to shut the hell up. But then she pulled out a small laptop from behind her back. "I've got Kai on videoconference for you."

"Really?" Hunter's guarded skepticism warred with a flicker of hope.

"I thought you could use another friendly face," Kate said, opening the laptop and tapping on the trackpad. "Not that you're lacking in that department. You have a good support system in those three."

The screen flickered to life, and there was Kai, seated in a room Hunter couldn't place. The background was blurry, a generic digital fuzz that gave away little. Kai's warm, easy smile filled the screen, and for a moment, the sterile chill of the medical lab seemed to fade.

Kate stepped back, her figure disappearing into the shadowed edges of the room, her presence reduced to a faint silhouette.

"Hunter," Kai's voice, steady and familiar, washed over him like a balm. "How are you holding up?"

Hunter sagged against the bed, his defenses faltering. "Could be better. They've got me hooked up like a damn lab experiment."

Kai chuckled softly. "Sounds about right."

Hunter's lips twitched into a reluctant smile before reality crashed back in. "I'm serious, Kai. It's bad. Worse than before."

Kai leaned closer to the camera, his expression softening. "I know. I can't imagine how hard this has been. But you're not alone. You've got people who care about you. Mugan, Ife. Slicer..."

"And Gibson," Hunter added, his voice trailing off as he searched Kai's face for reassurance.

Kai's hesitation was subtle but enough to stir suspicion. "Exactly," he said at last. "You've got Gibson. He's been there for you through everything. Maybe... maybe it's time to focus on that."

Hunter's brows knit together. "What are you saying?"

Kai's gaze dropped, his confident demeanor slipping. "I've been thinking a lot about us, Hunter. About what's best for you. And I think you need to let go of... us. At least for now."

The words landed like a punch to the gut. Hunter stared at the screen, disbelief etched across his face. "You can't mean that."

"I do." Kai's voice was soft, almost apologetic. "I love you, Hunter. But right now, you need stability. Someone who can ground you."

"That's not your decision to make!" Hunter's voice cracked, anger and heartbreak spilling out.

Kai's image flickered slightly, the connection briefly disrupted. "I'm trying to help you," he insisted. "Please, Hunter. Trust me."

Hunter's jaw tightened. "No. You don't get to decide what I need. You're hiding something. I can see it."

The flicker returned, and for the briefest moment, the clarity of Kai's face sharpened. The warmth in his eyes dimmed, replaced by a calculating glint that didn't belong. Hunter's heart dropped, but before he could manage another word, the screen went dark.

Behind him, Kate's voice cut through the silence. "I'll give you some time to process."

Hunter didn't turn to look at her. His eyes remained fixed on the laptop, the frost around him creeping outward as his heartache bled into his powers. He barely registered the faintest flicker of a smirk on Kate's lips as she quietly left the room.

Caeden Taylor IV reclined in his opulent office, a smirk tugging at his lips.

He was almost identical to Kai in appearance, but the differences were striking to those who would have known better. Where Kai's face radiated warmth and youthful optimism, Caeden's bore the marks of age and calculation. Lines etched his features, giving him the look of a man in his late forties who had lived several lifetimes too many. His dark hair, streaked with silver, was neatly combed back, and his piercing eyes carried none of Kai's openness. Instead, they gleamed with a predatory intelligence, sharp and unyielding.

His voice, when he spoke, was deeper and carried a weight that Kai's never could. Each word seemed to hold layers of intent, as if carefully measured for maximum effect. He was a man who exuded authority, the kind of presence that commanded rooms and brought armies to their knees. Even his posture–relaxed, yet unmistakably poised–hinted at someone who was always in control, always several steps ahead.

A computer alert indicated an incoming teleconference call. Caden accepted the call, and Kate's face reappeared. She appeared to be back in the lecture hall of the Alaskan medical complex.

"You were right," Caeden said, his voice a touch deeper than Kai's. "He's fracturing. It won't take much more."

Kate's head tilted. "Your performance was convincing. But are you sure about this? There's a fine line between breaking him and making him dangerous."

"Dangerous to them, not us," Caeden replied, steepling his fingers. "Every fracture brings him closer to severing from their control."

"And from Kai," Kate added, her tone tinged with irony.

Caeden's smirk widened. "That was the easiest part. They were always doomed. Their bond is too raw to survive."

Kate arched a brow but didn't press further. "What's next?"

Caeden's eyes glimmered as he leaned forward, tapping on a nearby holographic projection of The Order's hierarchy. "We move the next piece into position. By the time Hunter realizes the truth, it'll be too late for Kai—or him—to stop me."

Noah's office was a cluttered sanctuary of organized chaos. Schematics and diagrams covered the walls, their glowing lines pulsing faintly in the dim light. Books—both ancient and modern—were stacked in precarious towers around the room, and a holographic projector floated idle in the center. Gibson stepped carefully over cables and stray gadgets, his eyes landing on the sleek computer at the edge of Noah's desk.

"Hope you don't mind me borrowing this, Noah," Gibson muttered to the empty room, already powering up the machine.

The interface responded instantly to his touch, its sleek design glowing faintly as it synced with the realm's network. With a few quick commands, Gibson pulled up the portal bridge—a secure link to access files from the home realm. He hesitated, his fingers hovering over the keys as an unfamiliar pang of guilt washed over him, which he quickly discounted. He couldn't stay in the dark any longer.

A few keystrokes later, Hunter's medical records appeared on the screen. Gibson's breath hitched as he scanned the files. Diagnoses, treatment plans, and therapists' notes painted a grim picture. The words blurred together—"depressive episodes," "post-traumatic stress," "self-destructive tendencies."

But it was the most recent entry that made his stomach drop, a notation made by Dr. Mugan:

"Patient exhibits increasing signs of emotional dysfunction tied to powers activation. High risk of psychological destabilization. Recommended: heightened monitoring and separation from triggering influences."

The timestamp was only a month old.

Gibson's hands tightened into fists as a cold realization settled over him. This was only based on his *vampiric* powers - not the newly emerging *demonic* side of him.

"Damn it, Hunter," Gibson whispered, his voice thick with anger and guilt. "Why didn't you tell me?"

His gaze lingered on the screen, on the detached clinical notes that reduced Hunter's struggles to bullet points and risk assessments. For a moment, he felt utterly powerless, as if the divide between their worlds was more than just physical.

The restaurant Noah had chosen was nestled in a quiet corner of the downtown district, its amber-lit interior exuding a cozy charm that contrasted the sleek, mirrored buildings outside. Noah sat across from Al at a small wooden table, their plates half-empty between them. The low hum of a piano mingled with the quiet murmur of nearby conversations, but Noah was barely aware of it.

Al was mid-sentence, talking about something related to his work—maybe a debate he'd had with a co-worker at the store—but Noah's mind was elsewhere. The advice Kai had given him earlier still weighed heavily on his chest, coiling into a knot of guilt he couldn't ignore any longer.

"Noah?" Al's voice broke through his reverie. "You've been staring at your drink for, like, five minutes. Are you okay?"

Noah blinked and looked up, meeting Al's sharp green eyes. He forced a weak smile. "Yeah, sorry. I was just... thinking."

Al leaned back, his expression softening but still cautious. "You've been doing that a lot lately. What's going on?"

Noah hesitated, his fingers idly tracing the rim of his glass. "I've been trying to figure out how to say this," he began slowly. "It's about us."

Al's brow furrowed, but he didn't interrupt.

"When we first started getting serious, I told you about Albert," Noah said, his voice measured. "Your counterpart. I explained how he..." Noah paused, swallowing hard. "How he was someone I cared for deeply. And how he died."

Al nodded, his expression neutral. "I remember. You said you didn't want to treat me like I was him."

"I did say that," Noah admitted, his gaze dropping to the table. "And I meant it. But I've been questioning whether I've lived up to that promise. I need to be honest with you, Al–because I don't think I have."

Al tilted his head slightly, his eyes narrowing. "Are you saying you've been seeing him in me? That I've just been... a stand-in?"

Noah flinched at the bluntness but didn't look away. "At first, yeah. I didn't want to admit it–not to you, not even to myself–but it felt like a second chance. You reminded me of him in so many ways. The way you talk, the way your mind works... It was comforting. And I hate that, because you're not Albert. You're you, and you deserve better than being someone's crutch."

The silence that followed felt like it stretched forever. Al's gaze was steady, unreadable, and it took all of Noah's willpower not to fill it with nervous babbling.

Finally, Al leaned forward, resting his arms on the table. "So, let me ask you this," he said quietly. "When you look at me now, is it still him you see?"

Noah's chest tightened. He exhaled slowly, gathering his thoughts. "No," he said, his voice firm. "At first, maybe. But over time... I've gotten to know *you*. The way you argue over the smallest details, how you get that spark in your eye when you're onto something new, the way you... make me laugh even when I don't feel like it. Those are things that are yours, Al. Not his. And I've fallen for those things. For *you*."

Al studied him for a long moment, the tension in his shoulders softening. "You sure about that?"

Noah nodded. "I am. But I needed to tell you the truth—because if you feel like I've treated you as anything less than your own person, you deserve to call me out for it."

A small smile tugged at the corner of Al's mouth. "You're a complicated guy, you know that?"

Noah huffed a quiet laugh. "You don't know the half of it."

Al's smile grew. "Well, for what it's worth... I don't think you're lying. And I appreciate you telling me, even if it's messy. Relationships are messy." He leaned back, crossing his arms. "But just so we're clear—I expect you to fall for me *for me* from now on. No ghosts allowed."

Noah managed a genuine smile for the first time that evening. "Deal."

Slicer paced the perimeter of the common room, his movements fluid but restless, like a predator caged in an unfamiliar territory. Ife sat cross-legged on the floor, meticulously sorting through her medical supplies, while Mugan leaned against the wall, his arms crossed as he watched Slicer with quiet intensity.

"I don't like her," Slicer said abruptly, breaking the silence.

"Kate?" Ife asked, without looking up.

"Yeah, Kate." Slicer stopped pacing and turned to face them. "There's something off about her. I can't explain it, but I can't get a read on her. Even with my senses, I've got nothing—no smell that matches her words, no tone that gives her away. It's like she's... empty. Or too well-practiced."

Mugan tilted his head in contemplation. "You're saying she's masking herself?"

"Maybe," Slicer admitted, his brow furrowing. "But it's more than that. Even people who are good at hiding things slip up now and then. She doesn't. It's like she's always in control, always playing a part. And that makes me doubt her even more."

Ife stood up. "That's fair. She's not exactly forthcoming about her intentions, and she's certainly not warm. But what are we supposed to do about it? She's got the upper hand here, and we don't have anything solid to go on."

Slicer growled softly, the frustration evident in his voice. "I know. I just don't trust her. And with Hunter in the state he's in, we can't afford to ignore the possibility that she's working an angle we can't see."

Mugan uncrossed his arms and took a step forward. "I don't trust her either, but Ife's right. Without proof, we can't confront her. All we can do is stay vigilant."

"Vigilance isn't enough," Slicer snapped. "Hunter's vulnerable, and she's got her claws in him. We need to do more than just watch."

Ife placed a calming hand on Slicer's arm, her touch grounding. "I get it, Slicer. Believe me, I do. But right now, the best thing we can do is be there for him. Focus on helping him stabilize, physically and emotionally. Whatever Kate's up to, she can't control the bond we have with him."

Slicer's tension eased slightly, but his frown remained. "You're right. He needs us. But every time we try to get close, she's there. Blocking us, redirecting him. It's like she's trying to isolate him."

"Maybe she is," Mugan said, his voice low. "But until we can figure out why, we have to work around her. Find ways to reach Hunter without tipping her off."

Their conversation was interrupted by the sudden beep of an intercom. Kate's voice crackled through the system, smooth and impersonal. "Slicer, Ife, Mugan. I need you in the briefing room immediately. Hunter's recovery is being monitored, and he won't be available for visitors until further notice. Your cooperation is expected."

The three exchanged tense glances, the unspoken message clear: Kate was tightening her grip.

"She's cutting us off," Slicer muttered, his jaw tightening. "She knows we're onto her."

"Then we adapt," Ife said firmly, rising to her feet. "Kate might think she's in control, but she underestimates how much we care about Hunter. We'll find a way to help him, no matter what."

Mugan nodded in agreement. "For now, we play along. But we don't lose sight of the bigger picture."

As they filed out of the room, a quiet determination settled over the group. Kate's machinations might have given her the upper hand for now, but Slicer, Ife, and Mugan weren't about to back down. They'd find a way to protect Hunter, even if it meant working in the shadows.

14
BENEATH THE FROST LINE

Slicer sat alone in the dimly lit corner of the common room, the faint hum of distant conversations muffled by the thick stone walls. The faint scent of aged wood and smoke lingered in the air. His phone was cradled between his ear and shoulder, his fingers drumming an anxious rhythm on the table. The voice on the other end of the line was hurried and tense, laden with the weight of unwelcome news.

"We've got something solid," the voice said, cutting through the static. "The shipments–demon venom–two different sources confirmed. And Kate Coupland's name came up. She's been in contact with one of the main distributors."

Slicer's jaw tightened, his instincts screaming that this was the missing puzzle piece. His eyes scanned the room, as though expecting the shadows to shift with the weight of the revelation. "You're sure it's her?"

"As sure as we can be without a confession. She's playing it smart–using proxies, keeping her name out of the ledgers. But the connections are there."

Slicer leaned back in his chair, running a hand through his hair. "Damn it," he muttered. "This fits too well with what's been going on here. But she's got us boxed in."

"You need backup?"

"Not yet," Slicer replied. "I've gotta handle this from the inside first. But I'll keep you in the loop."

He ended the call and stared at the phone, debating his next move. After a moment's hesitation, he dialed Kai. The line rang once, twice, then went to voicemail. Frustrated, he tried Gibson next, but the call didn't connect at all, the fractured network of the realm adding another obstacle.

"Figures," he muttered, tossing the phone onto the table. His frustration gnawed at him, but beneath it, a seed of doubt began to grow. If Kate really was involved, then the stakes were even higher than they'd imagined. Without the others' support, he'd have to tread carefully.

Kate sat alone in a private room, a stark contrast to the bustling medical lab she had just left. The room was sparsely decorated, functional but devoid of personality, much like the woman herself. The only adornment was a sleek, high-tech communicator resting on the polished surface of her desk. She reached for it, her movements precise and deliberate, and activated a secure channel.

"It's me," she said softly, her tone carrying none of the warmth she had used with Hunter mere moments ago. This voice was colder, clipped. The kind of voice that gave orders, not reassurances.

The communicator crackled for a moment before the distorted voice of Caeden Taylor IV responded. "Report."

"The prime subject is stable," Kate replied, her eyes narrowing. "But the frost phenomena are intensifying. His resistance is... concerning. He hasn't taken the stabilizer yet, and there's no guarantee he will."

"You've always been persuasive," the voice said, laced with an edge of sarcasm. "Make him take it. We need him under control before the next phase begins."

Kate's lips pressed into a thin line. "I'm managing it. But there's another issue. Slicer has made contact with his network back in the Home Realm. They're connecting dots faster than expected. He's already suspicious of me."

The voice on the other end hissed, a sound that could have been static or irritation. "Can he be neutralized?"

"Not without drawing attention," Kate said, shaking her head slightly. "The others are watching too closely. Ife and Mugan are protective of Hunter, and Kai..." She paused, her expression hardening.

"Then accelerate the timeline," the voice interrupted sharply. "If they're closing in, we need to act before they can mount a defense. Ensure the venom shipments are ready to move. And keep the prime subject contained Neutralize it if you must. Do whatever it takes."

Kate's jaw tightened. "Understood. But if this falls apart—"

"It won't," the voice snapped. "Not if you do your job. Remember what's at stake."

The line went dead, leaving Kate staring at the blank screen. She set the communicator down carefully. For a moment, she sat in silence, her fingers drumming softly against the desk. Then she stood, her movements fluid and controlled, and left the room.

In the hallway, her expression shifted seamlessly back to the composed, caring professional everyone believed her to be. But behind her eyes, a storm brewed, colder and more dangerous than any frost Hunter could conjure.

Kai stood outside the door to Hunter II's quarters at Neptunes, his fingers brushing the edge of the wood as he hesitated. The meeting had been a long time coming, but now that he was here, uncertainty crept in. He took a deep breath and knocked twice.

The door opened almost immediately, revealing Hunter II—his hair slightly unkempt and dotted with dye jobs of black, red, and pink. His eyes held a guarded intensity that set him apart.

"Kai," Hunter II said, stepping aside to let him in. "Been wondering when you'd show up. His other 'other half' was here not too long ago."

Kai entered the room. He'd been here before, but this time he took more notice of the mish-mash of decorations. Mostly every piece of art or poster was one featuring Hunter II and his band. It gave off vibes of a self-aggrandizing shrine, a stark contrast to the warmth he'd known with Hunter Prime. "I wanted to check in," Kai said, his voice steady but cautious. "And to talk."

Hunter II leaned against the wall, crossing his arms. "About what? Flower arranging? Decoupage? Or something more specific?"

Kai chuckled lightly, though there was no humor in it. "Both, I guess. You and Hunter... you're different in some ways, but there's a lot of overlap too. I think you could help each other."

Hunter II raised an eyebrow. "Help each other? How?"

Kai met his gaze earnestly. "His powers are spiraling. He's struggling to keep himself together. You're... I can't believe I'm saying this, given our history, but you're stable, grounded. I think if you spent time together, he could find some balance. And maybe, in turn, he'd get some perspective on your own journey."

Hunter II's jaws softened, though skepticism lingered in his eyes. "You think it's that simple? Just two versions of the same guy hanging out and magically fixing each other?"

"Not simple," Kai admitted. "But worth trying. You've both been through hell. Maybe you're the only ones who can truly understand each other."

Hunter II looked away, his gaze distant. "I'll think about it. But don't expect me to be a miracle cure."

Kai's communicator buzzed as he left Hunter II's quarters, the fragmented message from Slicer flashing across the screen: "Venom... Kate... dangerous... be careful..."

Kai's stomach dropped. He tried to respond, but the connection failed. He stared at the screen, the weight of the message pressing down on him. With so many bombshells being levied at his feet, where to start? What to focus on? His stomach growled, and he remembered— *I can eat human food in this realm.* He headed in search of a restaurant, hoping food would give him the stamina to figure out his next move.

Kate took the single pill out of the container, the sterile white surface gleaming faintly in the dim light of the medical lab. She held it out to Hunter, her smile practiced but warm. "I know, it's as big as a horse pill," she said with a wry chuckle, her tone disarmingly casual. "But I figured you would prefer that to any more needles and injections."

Hunter eyed the pill, his jaw tightening. The room seemed unnaturally quiet, the hum of machinery fading into the background as his thoughts churned. He glanced at Kate, her friendly smile sending one message, yet exuding a practiced patience that set him further on edge.

"Will it... work?" he asked, his voice hesitant.

Kate's smile didn't falter. "It's designed to stabilize your powers. Nothing invasive, just a quick and effective solution. You'll feel better in no time."

But Hunter hesitated, his fingers twitching at his sides. The doubts whispered louder now—about Kate, about the pill, about everything she represented. His gaze flickered to her hand, still holding the pill, and for the briefest moment, he felt the frost creep across his fingertips, a visceral reminder of his fractured control.

"Hunter," Kate said softly, her tone dipping into something almost maternal. "This is for your own good. You need to trust me."

And still, he hesitated.

15
FIRST CONTACT

The lanterns outside Grossman's Provisions flickered in the balmy evening breeze, casting long, jittering shadows across the dusty street. Austin was bustling for a town on the cusp of the 20th century, the faint clatter of horseshoes mingling with the hum of conversation. Caeden stepped through the door, the faint creak of the wooden floorboards beneath his polished boots drawing a brief glance from the shopkeeper.

Mr. Grossman, a stout man with a bushy white mustache and sharp blue eyes, looked up from behind the counter where he was tallying a ledger. "Good evening, stranger," he greeted, his voice warm but tinged with curiosity. "What can I do for you?"

Caeden smiled, happy to be greeted by a friendly voice. "Good evening. I heard you might need an extra set of hands around here. I'm new to town and looking for work." His tone was smooth, practiced, a melody of sincerity and charm.

Grossman studied him for a moment, taking in the clean-cut appearance, the slightly too-pale complexion, and the air of mystery that seemed to cling to him. "Well, as it happens, I've been thinking about hiring a night watchman. Times being what they are, you never know who might come sneaking around after hours. You any good with your hands?"

"I can manage stock, keep an eye on things, and handle trouble if it comes to it," Caeden replied, meeting Grossman's gaze with an unwavering steadiness. He was wondering if he might need to try influencing him. He prepared to focus himself so that he could engage the power at a moment's notice.

But he needn't have worried. "Fair enough. Start tonight, and we'll see how you do. Pay's a dollar a week, and you'll get your supper here," Grossman said, closing the ledger with a decisive thump. "Name's Sam Grossman, by the way."

"Caeden," he replied simply, shaking the offered hand. Grossman's grip was firm but not overbearing.

As the hours slipped by, Caeden proved himself capable, unloading crates of flour and jars of preserves with ease that belied his lean frame. He moved with an efficiency that drew no suspicion but spoke of years of experience beyond his youthful appearance. Grossman, impressed, watched from the counter as Caeden stacked barrels of salted pork as if they weighed nothing at all.

"You've certainly got a knack for this," Grossman remarked as the clock struck ten. He handed Caeden a steaming plate of stew from the back kitchen. "Sit, eat. You've earned it."

Caeden took the plate with a grateful smile, but as Grossman turned to pour himself a drink, he subtly tipped the stew onto a napkin-lined bucket hidden beneath the table. When Grossman returned, Caeden had the spoon in his hand, stirring the empty plate as though finishing the last bite.

"Thank you," Caeden said, settling the plate aside. Grossman took a seat across from him, wiping his hands on a well-worn apron.

"You're looking for a place to stay, I take it," Grossman said, watching him closely. "Mrs. Howe runs a boarding house over on Hill Road. Good woman, keeps a clean house. I reckon she'll have a room to spare if you don't mind sharing space with a few other boarders."

"That's more than kind of you to suggest," Caeden replied with a slight nod. "I'll pay her a visit."

Grossman's lips formed into a half-smile. "Austin's a close-knit place, Caeden. Folks here look out for each other. You seem like you'll fit right in, as long as you're not one of those troublemakers the Railroad Ripper's got everyone worried about."

Caeden's expression remained neutral, though the mention of the Ripper set his mind churning. "I've heard talk," he said carefully. "Seems like a grim affair."

"Grim, all right," Grossman muttered, shaking his head.

Caeden leaned forward slightly, lowering his voice to a tone of quiet curiosity. "Have your customers said anything that doesn't sound like straw gossip? Perhaps something the papers haven't mentioned?"

Grossman's brows furrowed as he thought for a moment. "There's always talk. Some folks think the Ripper's got a grudge against the railroad, others say it's someone hiding in plain sight. A few mentioned hearing strange sounds near the railyard late at night, like metal scraping and footsteps where there shouldn't be any. But you know how it is–folks' imaginations run wild when they're scared."

"Strange sounds, you say," Caeden mused, filing the detail away. "Anyone in particular worth speaking to?"

Grossman shrugged. "Maybe Old Billy. He's been working near the railyard for years and says he's seen things. Could be worth a chat if you don't mind a bit of rambling."

"Thank you. That's helpful," Caeden replied with a small nod. He stood, ready to finish the night's tasks. The Railroad Ripper might have terrorized the town, but he was a predator of a different sort. And now, he was in the heart of it, slipping seamlessly into the role of protector while the hunt began.

When Grossman decided he would retire at his own home in the outlay behind the store just after midnight, he showed Caeden to the storage cellar, a cool, windowless space beneath the shop, lined with shelves of preserved goods and barrels of grain. "You can rest here until you get something more permanent," he offered. "Door locks from the inside, so you'll have your privacy."

Caeden nodded appreciatively. "Thank you. This will do perfectly." The lack of windows suited him more than Grossman realized.

Just after sundown the following day, Caeden made his way to Mrs. Howe's boarding house on Hill Road. The two-story structure had a welcoming, if slightly weathered, appearance, with whitewashed walls and a wrap-around porch. Mrs. Howe, a matronly woman with sharp eyes and an air of authority, greeted him at the door, having been alerted earlier in the day by Mr. Grossman that Caeden would be calling on her.

"I heard you've a room to let," Caeden said with a courteous bow of his head.

"Indeed," Mrs. Howe replied, studying him. "We've got rules here, Mr. Caeden. No trouble, no late-night comings and goings, and rent's due every week without fail."

"That's agreeable," he said smoothly. "Might I ask about the other boarders?"

She hesitated, then gave a small smile. "Curious sort, aren't you? Let's see. There's Mr. Harvey Jenkins, works for the railroad; Miss Eliza Trilling, a schoolteacher; and Mr. Milton Hargrove, who keeps to himself mostly. All respectable folk."

"I'll keep that in mind," Caeden replied, handing her the first week's rent. After inspecting the modest but clean room, he set about unpacking his meager belongings. He made a mental note to observe the other boarders closely; one of them could be more than they seemed.

After getting settled, he made his way to the bathroom, located just next to his own quarters. The bath, Caeden found, was greatly out of proportion to the rest of the room, which seemed to have been another living area or something else before the home was converted for multiple private residents. Plumbing was installed as an afterthought, and pipes lay exposed against the walls. They were tied haphazardly to a washbasin and a siphon toilet that sat uncomfortably close to the tub itself. Thankfully, the darkness of night helped hide them.

The gentle orange flicker of lamp light aided Caeden find the washing sponge within the water. He finished up and pulled the stopper out of the water. Stepping gingerly out of the tub and wrapping himself in a terrycloth towel, Caeden stepped to the washbasin. Looking in the mirror, he opened his mouth and let his fangs descend a few times. Each time they clicked into place, he sighed a little, as if hopeful that the next time he tried, the fangs would simply not do so.

His eyes wandered to a pail sitting next to the commode seat. Several editions of old newspapers sat, rolled or folded, as ersatz toilet paper.

"MURDER!" The thick black strokes of the headline glared out from the neatly-folded square of paper. Intrigued, Caeden picked the paper out from the pail and unfolded it.

"RIPPER STRIKES CITY." The subheadline was in the same type but in smaller, yet still attention-grabbing size. "The Railroad Ripper, long derided by officials as vulgar tall tales shared among the vagabonds that ride the rails to and from our fair city, is legend no longer.

"Earlier to-day, San Antonio Sheriff Herbert Peck discovered the body of a woman near the freight depot on the south end of town. Peck told this reporter the condition of the body was found 'in a most horrid state.' Bystanders who witnessed the scene noted the wretched woman 'barely had anything that could be presently considered a face.' Peck said there were various blade wounds across other areas of the body.

"Peck said he is now willing to accept that there may indeed be a serial killer visiting San Antonio and other Texas cities via the railways. There has been a series of a dozen or so similar killings throughout our state and into Oklahoma over the past three years. There has been no common link to any of the victims other than that they lived near a local Texas Union Railway depot station. Peck added that it seems each new victim is dispatched in increasingly more violent fashion.

"Anyone with information as to the identity of the woman or the killer is urged to contact law enforcement as swiftly as possible."

Returning to Grossman's later that evening, Caeden stepped inside to find a small crowd gathered. Old Billy, a wiry man with sun-leathered skin and an air of urgency, was speaking animatedly to Grossman and a few other patrons.

"Telling you, I heard it again last night!" Billy exclaimed, gesturing with a bony hand. "Metal scraping, like something bein' dragged, and footsteps–heavy ones –near the west yard. No one ever sees nothin', but it's there, I'm tellin' ya!"

The others exchanged dubious glances, but Caeden's ears pricked at the mention of the west yard. He leaned casually against the counter, appearing disinterested while he listened closely.

"You ever notice," Billy continued, lowering his voice, "it only happens after the late freight comes through? Like clockwork, I tell ya."

That detail snagged in Caeden's mind. A pattern tied to the freight schedule? The others dismissed Billy's account as the ramblings of a dithering old man, but Caeden knew better. Sometimes the truth hid in plain sight, dismissed by those unwilling to look closer.

As the crowd dispersed, Caeden approached Grossman. "Mind if I have a word with Billy?" he asked.

Grossman chuckled. "If you've the patience for him, be my guest."

Caeden nodded and stepped outside, catching up with Billy as he shuffled down the street. "Billy," he called, his tone friendly. "Got a moment? I'd like to hear more about what you've seen."

Billy paused, squinting up at him. "You one of them newspaper fellas?"

"Nothing like that," Caeden assured him. "Just someone who listens." Caeden's calm demeanor seemed to put Billy at ease, and the older man leaned heavily on his cane as he nodded.

"Well, I don't reckon many folks care to listen these days," Billy grumbled, his voice gravelly but steady. "You said you're interested in what I've seen?"

Caeden offered a faint smile. "That's right. You mentioned strange sounds by the west yard after the late freight comes through. Could you tell me more?"

Billy rubbed his chin thoughtfully, glancing up and down the street as if checking for eavesdroppers. "Ain't much to tell that I ain't already said," he began, his voice lowering. "But it's like this–every few nights, right after that late freight rolls in, there's noises. Metal, like chains or a blade bein' dragged, and footsteps, heavy ones, like boots hittin' the ground. I've even caught a glimpse of shadows movin' where no one should be."

"Shadows?" Caeden pressed, his tone remaining neutral.

"Yessir," Billy replied. "Tall, too, taller than any man I've known. And it's not just the shadows that don't sit right. There's a smell sometimes–iron, like blood, and something... sour."

That gave Caeden pause. The description was vivid enough to stir his curiosity further. "Have you ever tried to get closer? To see who or what it might be?"

Billy snorted. "Son, I may be old, but I ain't stupid. Whatever's out there... it ain't natural. I told the rail bosses once, but they waved me off, said it's probably stray dogs or hobos passin' through. But I know what I heard–and smelled."

Caeden nodded thoughtfully. "Thank you, Billy. I appreciate you sharing that with me."

Billy squinted at him again. "You seem different, mister. Most folks just laugh me off."

"I've found that truth often hides in the places people overlook," Caeden said cryptically. "Stay safe, Billy. If you notice anything else, let me know."

Billy gave a small nod, tipping his battered hat before shuffling off into the night. Caeden watched him go, his mind already piecing together the details. The late freight, the sounds, the shadows–it was too deliberate to be random. The mention of a metallic scent, possibly blood, was especially damning.

He would have to investigate the west yard, but not yet. Patience was a predator's greatest ally, he remembered Olivia teaching him.

For now, he realized as he spied a clock in a nearby shop window, he had a shop to tend to. With a smile at a job well done, Caeden turned back toward Grossman's and trotted back to its front doors, picking up a broom leaning against the entrance and sweeping the board planks with a sense of satisfaction.

Under the warm glow of the lanterns inside Grossman's Provisions, the shop was alive with the bustle of late evening customers. Caeden moved about with practiced ease, sweeping the floorboards, stacking jars of pickled vegetables, and ensuring the shelves were tidy. His sharp senses, however, were attuned to every conversation and every face.

The bell above the door jingled, and a man stepped in, drawing the attention of the room. He was tall and broad-shouldered, his face shadowed beneath the brim of a wide hat. His clothes were dusty, the kind of grime that suggested long hours spent on the rails or in the wilderness. A faint metallic tang wafted in as he moved past Caeden, sharper than the scent of sweat or dirt.

"Evening," the man grunted, his voice low and gruff. He approached the counter, his heavy boots thudding against the floor with each step. Grossman looked up from his inventory with a polite, if cautious, nod.

"Evening to you. What'll it be?" Grossman asked.

"Coffee. Flour. And I'll take one of those knives you keep in the glass case," the man said, his eyes flicking briefly toward Caeden, then away again. His gaze was unsettling—sharp and calculating, like someone used to assessing threats.

Caeden kept sweeping but positioned himself where he could observe the interaction. The man's movements were deliberate, almost rehearsed, as though he were accustomed to being watched.

Grossman unlocked the case and produced a hunting knife, its blade gleaming under the lamplight. "That'll be two dollars," he said, setting it on the counter.

The man pulled a crumpled bill from his pocket and dropped it on the counter. As Grossman counted the money, Caeden's attention sharpened. The man's hands were rough and scarred, his fingernails lined with dirt—and, if Caeden wasn't mistaken, there was something darker beneath one of them, almost blackened, like dried blood.

"Anything else?" Grossman asked, his tone polite but clipped.

The man shook his head. "That'll do."

As he turned to leave, Caeden caught another whiff of that metallic tang. It wasn't the knife—it was coming from the man himself, faint but unmistakable. The man adjusted his hat and strode toward the door, his boots clumping against the floor with the same heavy rhythm Billy had described.

Before he stepped out, Caeden called out casually, "You're new around here, aren't you? Haven't seen you in town before."

The man paused, his hand on the doorframe. He glanced over his shoulder. "Just passing through," he said curtly, then stepped outside into the night.

As the door swung shut, Grossman exhaled softly. "Don't much like that one," he muttered, shaking his head. "Been in a few times now. Always late at night, always the same strange air about him."

Caeden set the broom aside, his thoughts racing. "Do you know his name?"

Grossman frowned, thinking. "He said it once. Miller, maybe? Or Milton. Something like that. Claims he's been working odd jobs along the railway. Why?"

"No reason," Caeden said smoothly. "Just curious."

But it wasn't just curiosity. The man's mannerisms, his scent, and the heavy footfalls all aligned too closely with Billy's description. Caeden resolved to keep an eye out for him–and to investigate the west yard sooner than planned. Whatever was happening in Austin, he had a feeling this man might be tied to it in more ways than one.

16

AVALANCHE

Hunter swallowed the pill with a labored gulp. It tasted bitter and faintly metallic.

Kate smiled at him warmly as he took the pill. "Very good," she said with an air of simplicity. "Soon we'll have you packed back up and ready to go." She swung her legs around and hopped out of the stool. Hunter's eyes followed her as she strode to the exit door. As he watched her toss the prescription bottle into the wastebasket, his vision began to cloud. He suddenly felt as if a huge weight had been placed upon his head.

"Sleep now, Hunter," Kate said, still facing the door. She opened the door and stepped out. "Forever," she added with a cold, gleeful refrain, shutting the door and locking it tight.

Alarmed, Hunter tried to bolt forward, but the effects of the medicine were working at a remarkable pace. He had to focus his eyes on the hospital bed, will his arms to clamp onto the railing, force his body up, and land his feet on the cold tile floor.

He fell almost immediately, his head hitting the cold floor. He saw five bright stars burst in front of his line of vision. With a huff of effort, he crawled the few meters from the bed to the wastebasket by the door. He plunged one hand into the trash and pulled out the bottle. His vision deteriorating, he cupped his free hand against his head, pushing against his eyes in a desperate attempt to see straight.

"Compounded materials," he read: "1500 milligrams diphenhydramine, 1500 milligrams ketamine, 500 milligrams benzodiazepine, 500 milligrams powdered silver."

This wasn't a 'horse pill,' Hunter realized... it was more like a horse *tranquilizer*! It was more than enough to likely *kill* a horse! And with powdered silver in the mix, he thought with horror...

The searing pain inside his gut began immediately, causing him to lurch over the wastebasket and grip the wire edges tightly. The silver was already eating away at his vampire flesh, sizzling at his undead organs.

Bathroom, Hunter thought, dropping the bottle with a clatter to the floor, lumbering his body on a continued crawl to the lavatory a few excruciating feet away. *I gotta vomit this shit up... fast...*

"Tsk, tsk, tsk," said an all-too-familiar voice. "Why turn your nose up at a gift like this?"

Hunter's field of vision narrowed and dimmed until it was pitch black. A tremendous surge of sensation washed over his body, as if he was being pulled by his hands and feet into a new position – and as far as he knew, he was.

"She's giving you your deepest, darkest desire," cooed his inner voice. "An end. A punctuation mark. End the sentence, close the chapter, throw the book into the fire!"

Hunter scrunched his face up, closing his eyes tightly. *Picture the commode,* he told himself. *Will yourself to move there – it's the only way.*

"The only *way*," hissed the dark, oily voice, "is to let the pill do its work and set me free!"

The hum of the break room fridge blended with the low murmur of conversation as Slicer, Mugan, and Ife leaned casually against the counter. Slicer tossed a sugar packet into the air, catching it with a practiced flick of his wrist.

"I'm telling you," Slicer said, grinning, "if you could shapeshift like me, you'd never need to worry about parking. I shift, hop out as a coyote, and bam–instant mobility."

Mugan raised an eyebrow as he poured a cup of coffee. Despite being a vampire, Mugan often had food and beverage near him, enjoying the smells that reminded him of human life. "You ever think about going bigger, though? Like a bear or something? Might make people think twice before cutting you off in traffic."

Slicer smirked. "Sure, if I want to terrify half the block. Coyotes are subtle. They blend in. Plus, it fits me– scrappy, resourceful, and damn good at surviving. It's why the coyote is my go-to shift."

"You do know coyotes aren't universally loved," Ife chimed in, her voice tinged with dry amusement as she stirred her tea. "You might want to rethink the 'fits me' part."

"I take it as a compliment," Slicer shot back, his grin widening. "Survival's an art, Ife. Can't be worrying about popularity contests when you're out in the wild."

"Fair," she replied, though the corners of her mouth twitched upward.

Mugan leaned against the counter, swirling his coffee. "Speaking of surviving," he said, "you wouldn't believe the kinds of characters that walk into the Electric Six back in Dallas. You get a front-row seat to humanity's finest, or maybe its weirdest."

"Listen, biker bars give you exactly that–and more" Slicer said, genuine curiosity in his tone.

"Of course," Mugan said, a hint of pride coloring his voice. "But E6 is more than just a nightclub–it's a hub. We've hosted everyone from local artists to people I swear have stepped out of a spy novel. It keeps things… interesting."

"Interesting's one way to put it," Ife said, raising an eyebrow. "And I'm guessing half your clientele doesn't even know about your other job."

Mugan chuckled. "They don't need to. Let's just say the Electric Six pulls its weight in more ways than one."

"I've been meaning to ask," Ife said, pointing at a sheath attached to a belt loop on Mugan's jeans. "When did you start carrying knives?"

Mugan's lips curled into a faint smile. "Oh, this? It's a little something I picked up in my studies. This blade was buried in a tomb older than The Order or The Crown." He popped the clasp and pulled gently on the handle.

"It's called an Estinal, and there's conflicting lore about it. Some books say it can transport demons back to their homes. Others say it can kill with a single thrust."

"That's... true about most knives, isn't it?" Slicer said.

Mugan frowned. "Well, yes... but I'm sure something this ornate that the craftsman gave a name to must have special properties when used on the right entity."

The lighthearted air shifted abruptly as all three agents' devices buzzed simultaneously. Slicer froze mid-sentence, glancing down. The playful grin on his face faded as he stared at the notification. "Wait... no way," he whispered, his voice uncharacteristically subdued.

"What's happening?" Ife's tone sharpened as she checked her own device. Her expression darkened, her usual calm fracturing.

"This can't be real," Mugan said, shaking his head, but his voice carried a hollow edge.

"No," Ife muttered. "He wouldn't in a million years..."

Slicer let out a shaky breath, his hand tightening around the counter's edge. "What does this mean? It's gotta be bad. Really bad."

The door swung open, and Kate entered with brisk, purposeful strides. Her gaze swept over the trio, analyzing their reactions to the news.

"You've seen it," she said, her voice steady but laced with urgency.

Mugan, Slicer, and Ife nodded in unison, too stunned to speak.

"My orders have come down, and you are to immediately leave," Kate instructed, her tone brooking no argument. "Report to your home offices. I am to stay here and oversee Hunter's medical care."

"But–" Mugan started, his voice heavy with protest.

"No arguments," Kate cut him off firmly. "We don't have time to debate. Go."

Exchanging uneasy glances, the three hesitated only for a moment before gathering their belongings and filing out of the room. As the door swung shut behind them, Kate exhaled softly, steeling herself as she turned toward the hallway leading to the medical ward.

The Other Realm moon hung low and ominous, casting a slightly green, silvery sheen over jagged peaks over the strange Dallas-like skyline. The cracked glass windows of Noah's office offered an even more skewed view of the cityscape, its jagged spires and eerie stillness making the realm's alien nature undeniable.

Noah paced the length of the room, his boots striking the tiled floor with sharp, deliberate steps.

"Kai, you don't understand," Noah said sharply, his tone bordering on exasperation.

Kai sat perched on the edge of a desk, arms crossed and brows furrowed. "No, Noah, *you* don't understand. Al isn't Albert. No matter how much you want him to be, he never will be."

Noah's fists clenched at his sides. "This isn't about Albert," he snapped. "Al is his own person. He's been invaluable here, helping us navigate this place."

Kai's expression softened, but his voice remained firm. "You're clinging to him because you haven't accepted Albert's death. You think if you can keep Al close, it somehow fills that hole."

Noah turned away, his jaw tight. "You don't know what you're talking about."

"I know grief when I see it," Kai said, standing now. "You've seen it blind *me*. I know it's blinding *you*. This isn't healthy, Noah. Let him go."

The sharp chime of Noah's device interrupted the tension. He pulled it from his pocket, frowning as he read the subject line. His breath caught.

"Oh my God. Calhoun," he murmured, his voice hollow.

"What about him?" Kai asked, his posture straightening.

Noah's eyes scanned the message, growing darker with each passing second. He read aloud, his voice trembling but resolute.

"'To all Order operatives: Supervisor Winston Calhoun has been confirmed deceased. Cause of death: homicide. A suspect has been identified. Capture and termination orders are now in effect for...'" Noah hesitated, his eyes flicking up to Kai.

"For *you*."

Kai's breath caught. "What?"

Noah shook his head, speaking firmly. "You've been here in the Other Realm with me all day. There's no way you could've done this."

Kai exhaled shakily. "Then why name me?"

Noah's jaw tightened as he glanced at the screen again. He turned it around to show Kai. There were a pair of images from what appeared to be closed circuit cameras from Calhoun's home. One showed Calhoun in a leather recliner, reading a newspaper, as a cloaked figure approached from behind.

The second image, taken moments later, showed the grisly aftermath – Calhoun, now slumped in the chair, bleeding profusely from the forehead - a railroad spike driven into his skull. Standing over him, with crystal clarity, appeared to be Kai.

Kai stepped forward. "We need to clear this up now. I need to get back–"

"Wait," Noah interrupted, holding up a hand. "You can't just go back. Gibson is the only one capable of helping you teleport, and until we understand what's going on, heading home makes you a sitting target."

Kai's hands clenched into fists at his sides. "So what? I just wait here until the Order sends someone after me?"

"I don't think they'll come here," Noah assured him. "Not yet. They'd have no reason to think you're in the Other Realm. We've got time to figure this out."

Kai nodded slowly, though the tension in his frame remained. "I need to contact Gibson."

Hunter pictured himself on his hands and knees in front of the toilet in the restroom. If he could picture doing it here, he probably *was* in reality there, he reasoned.

There was a horrid sounding *gurgle* coming from his stomach and a continued growing feeling of lethargy. *It would feel so nice to go to sleep...*

"Yesss," hissed the voice. "Sleep soundly." The voice sounded like a combination of the unwanted dark thoughts and the parting words of Kate as she locked him in the exam room. "Forever..."

Hunter tried his best to ignore. He continued to picture every time he'd been ill in his human life, every time he'd had a vomiting spell. He groaned as he imagined, but didn't experience the sensations he needed.

"I gave you every disorder, every mental illness," growled the voice. "You couldn't even *starve* yourself like you wanted to... you pathetic excuse for a human!"

"I'm... *not* human... anymore!" Hunter winced and writhed. He felt something *pop* inside his stomach. He was certain the silver was liquefying and expanding within him. He didn't have much time left.

The voice's taunting *did* give him an idea, though.

Hunter thought back to his freshman year of high school, when he was caught up in a spell of binging and purging. When it came time to make himself puke, there was a memory he'd always bring up that would make him queasy enough to want to vomit.

His eyes began to dilate and transmit beams of bright purple light.

The band hall...

Springtime...

All those crickets...

The school campus was catty-corner from a marshland and a breeding ground for crickets. Every spring, thousands and thousands of the insects would converge on school grounds. And kids wouldn't necessarily sidestep them.

Crickets began to appear all around Hunter by the hundreds. Their friendly chirp-chirping quickly became a deafening echo.

Every day the sidewalks would be littered with...
CRUNCH. CRUNCH. CRUNCH.

The carpet of crickets that would regularly enter the band hall became pressed and compressed over the course of the day by the heavy footsteps of a hundred school-age children, decimating virtually all of them. Cricket bodies cracked, popped, and burst, spreading pools of white coagulated guts and clear fluids in a grotesque palate of insect paint.

Serrated legs continued to twitch, far away from the bodies which once housed them.

Hunter saw himself kneeling in front of the exam room toilet at last, surrounded by the memories of a million cricket parts fermenting in the school day air.

Oh, gods, the smell, he remembered.

He put a hand over his fist as he pressed into his agonized gut. He pushed.

A partially-bisected cricket wriggled in panic, separating itself from the rest of its body.

Eggs oozed from the emaciated body of another.

Hunter pushed again. A wave of heat and nausea hit him and he retched, hanging his head over the toilet bowl. The splatter of vomit and chunks of dissolved flesh quickly overtook the imagined sounds of cricket chirps. This sight, not imagined, not projected, made it even easier to continue vomiting. It felt like he had a fire hose emptying out of his mouth.

Five hefty heaves later, Hunter collapsed backwards, his head hitting his arm as he pawed at the floor, welcoming its cold temperature.

He opened his eyes and waited.

Above him, the antiseptic white light of a medical room light fixture.

No smoke, no clouds.

No sounds around him, either.

Woozy, he pushed himself into an upright position. Convinced after a few moments that he had the strength to do so, he stood up.

He stepped to the sink next to the toilet, consciously avoiding the sight of the overfilled bowl, and opened his mouth.

Bile, froth, and streaks of red indicating leaking fluids continued to ooze out.

"Evermore," he mumbled, looking at his face in the mirror. "I've gotta get to some Evermore."

If he could get a couple of bottles down, maybe he could negate the effects of this pill. Then he could repair himself and regain his strength.

And then I can tear that bitch from limb to limb, he growled to himself.

He raced to the locked door, and with an enraged door, yanked it off its hinges, tossed it aside with a ferocious clatter.

17
WHITEOUT

The roar of the helicopter blades drowned out the ambient noise of the frigid Alaskan wilderness below. Mugan sat at the controls, his sharp gaze fixed on the storm-laden horizon as he steered the craft on a beeline for San Francisco. Ife and Slicer occupied the back seats, the tension between them palpable in the confined space. The dim light from the cockpit cast jagged shadows, which danced wildly over the tablet Ife held, showing a photograph documenting the death of their leader–and supposedly showing Kai committing the murder.

"I still can't believe it," Ife said, her voice tight with disbelief. "Winston... gone. And Kai? How could he...?"

"He didn't." Mugan's voice cut through the din, calm but resolute. His hands gripped the controls, his knuckles pale. "That's not Kai."

"But the evidence–the photograph..." Ife's voice wavered as she looked down at her hands. "Mugan, it's all pointing to him."

Slicer leaned forward, the orange-brown glint of his shapeshifter's eyes catching the dim light. "Don't believe this shit for a second," he said, his voice a low growl. "It's too neat, too convenient." His pointed to something on the photograph. "Here," he muttered, taking the tablet and using two fingers to zoom in on the picture.

"What is it?" Mugan asked, sparing a quick glance over his shoulder as he piloted the chopper.

Slicer pointed to a detail on the blurred figure of Kai in the photo. "That cufflink. Near his hand."

Ife leaned closer, squinting. The photograph showed Kai standing over Winston Calhoun's body. On Kai's wrist, partially obscured, was a cufflink engraved with an intricate sigil—one that shimmered faintly in the light. Unfortunately, coming from a closed-circuit security camera, the resolution was too blurry to see what the symbol was.

"What about it?" Ife asked.

"Hunter talks about Kai nonstop back at the bar," Slicer's voice dropped. "Kai hated jewelry. Said it was impractical."

Mugan's jaw tightened as he listened to the conversation.

"You think they set him up?" Ife whispered, her voice trembling.

"I'll bet you anything this was The Crown," Slicer continued. "We know they've worked with demons before. Maybe they found someone who looks enough like Kai, someone who could mimic him just enough to fool us."

"A doppelgänger?" Ife asked, her brow furrowing.

"Not quite," Slicer replied. "But hire some poor shlub, put them through whatever paces to radicalize them, if they weren't already inclined to kill, and you've got yourself a perfect scapegoat."

Mugan's hands tightened on the steering deck as the chopper shuddered from turbulence. "We need proof. Whatever this is, it's not just about Kai. It's about what comes next. For all of us."

"Right," Ife said, her voice barely audible over the hum of the blades. "This is clearly an attack on all of us. So what is our next move?"

Slicer grinned. His teeth almost seemed feral. "We hunt. Like we always do."

The helicopter continued on, as Mugan pushed it to its limits. Each of them sat silently the rest of the way, left to their own thoughts – each of them thinking it may not have been in Hunter's best interest to have been left behind.

The brown brick edifice of The Order's San Francisco offices was coming into view when Slicer's head snapped back, as an intense wave of panic that was not his own surged through him, his breath hitching in his throat. He gripped the edge of his seat, his sharp fingernails digging into the fabric.

"Hunter," he growled, his voice strained.

Mugan shot him a glance, his brow furrowing. "What's going on, mate?"

Ife blinked, confused. "Slicer? What's happening?"

Slicer didn't answer immediately. Instead, he closed his eyes, focusing on the blood bond's pull. The sensation was overwhelming—Hunter's distress radiated like a beacon, sharp and frantic.

"We were right to be worried about Hunter," Slicer reported. "He's in extreme pain."

Hundreds of miles and an entire dimension away, Kai staggered in an alleyway just outside a hotel he was about to check into, clutching his chest. His breath came in ragged gasps as Hunter's panic threatened to pull him under. "Damn it," he muttered, slamming a hand against the wall to steady himself.

"Kai." Noah's voice was full of concern as he grabbed Kai's arm in an attempt to steady him. "Is it Hunter?"

"Yeah," Kai replied, his voice tight. All he wanted at that moment was the ability to teleport just like his lover, so he could tend to his distress. But he knew that he could not – not while he stood accused of murdering Calhoun.

Kai leaned heavily against the brick wall of the alley, his breaths coming in short, painful gasps. Noah crouched beside him, his hand firm on Kai's shoulder. "You need to sit down," Noah urged, his voice steady despite the storm of emotions playing across his face.

Kai shook his head, teeth clenched. "Hunter's in trouble. I can feel it. It's like... like he's being torn apart from the inside."

"I get that," Noah said, his tone soft but unyielding. "But you won't help him by collapsing here."

Reluctantly, Kai allowed Noah to guide him to a crouched position against the wall. Noah's jacket was off in a flash, draped over Kai's trembling shoulders, despite the chill in the air.

Kai closed his eyes, trying to steady the overwhelming pull of the blood bond. His voice was low when he spoke again. "It's more than just pain, Noah. It's fear. Pure, unrelenting fear. I've never felt him like this before."

Noah sat beside him, their shoulders nearly touching. "What exactly do you feel through the bond?" he asked, his tone a mix of curiosity and concern.

"It's like... fragments of his emotions bleed into me. Pain, fear, sometimes even glimpses of his thoughts, but it's chaotic–like trying to piece together a shattered mirror." Kai's voice broke on the last word, and he dragged a hand through his hair. "And I can't do anything to help him."

"No, you can't... right *now*," Noah corrected gently. "But you will. *We* will. You're not in this alone, Kai."

For a moment, Kai's mask of stoic resolve cracked. He glanced at Noah, his amber eyes shining with unshed tears. "Why are you still here? You know the Dallas office, someone from The Order's going to contact you about my location and–"

"Because I know you didn't do it," Noah interrupted. His voice was firm, leaving no room for doubt. "And because I care about you. Simple as that."

Kai blinked, caught off guard by the certainty in Noah's words. He opened his mouth to respond, but the faint hum of a police siren in the distance snapped them both into focus.

"We can't stay here," Noah said, standing and offering Kai his hand. He used his other hand to smack the brick wall like he was patting a good friend on the back. "Let's get you inside this building instead of hanging around outside it, yeah?"

Kai took the offered hand, his grip firm despite his weariness. "But when this is over, when Hunter's safe, we're going to find out who did this. And they'll pay."

Noah nodded, a fierce determination lighting his eyes. "Damn right they will."

About ten blocks away from the hotel, at Neptunes, Gibson stood abruptly from his chair, the blood bond thrumming in his veins. He turned to Hunter II.

Hunter's duplicate leaned back against the bar, his arms crossed, his expression unreadable. "What's going on?"

"It's Hunter," Gibson said, pacing the room in a restless loop. "He's in trouble. I can feel it–it's like his pain is seeping into me."

Hunter II straightened, his gaze sharpening. "How bad?"

"Bad," Gibson replied. "It's like his entire body is on fire... mixing with extreme cold. And there's fear–he's terrified." He stopped pacing, turning to Hunter II with a mixture of frustration and desperation. "But I can't pinpoint him. I only know the general location. Have you ever been to Matthew Island, Alaska?"

Hunter II shook his head as a thoughtful frown crossed his features. "No, but I know it's pretty isolated. No matter--we'll have to bridge the gap."

"What do you mean?" Gibson asked, his brow furrowing.

Hunter II stepped forward, raising his hands in front of him, palms out. "Blood bonds aren't just passive connections, you know. If you focus, I can amplify them. Then we can teleport there. But it takes effort—and trust."

Gibson hesitated, then mirrored Hunter II's stance, their palms almost touching. "How do we do this?"

"Close your eyes," Hunter II instructed, his voice low and steady. "Focus on Hunter. Think of him—his presence, his energy. Let the bond guide you."

Gibson took a deep breath and closed his eyes. He concentrated on the pull of the bond, the faint hum that connected him to Hunter. Slowly, it grew louder, more distinct, like a thread winding tighter. He could feel Hunter's fear more acutely now, the sharp edge of it cutting into his thoughts.

"Good," Hunter II said softly. "Now hold onto that. I'll take care of the rest."

A strange sensation washed over Gibson, like a current of energy flowing between him and Hunter II. The air seemed to hum with power, and for a moment, he could almost see the bond—a glowing strand stretching out into the distance, pulsing with life.

The glow began to wrap itself around Gibson and the alternate-world Hunter. It began to crackle with electricity, arcing over the pair like a jump rope. The crackling accelerated, faster and faster. Then, a tremendous flash of light filled the room, and when it dissipated, they were gone.

Back in the helicopter, Slicer growled into his cell phone. "Yo, Piston. This is Slicer from the Texas pack. Listen, I need your guys to suit up. We've got a situation.

I need ya'll to meet me and a friend of mine up in Matthew Island. Yes, head out now."

Ife looked at him, alarmed. "What are you doing?"

"I'm going back," Slicer replied, his voice resolute. "And I'm calling in a pack I know over in Anchorage. They've got a boat and they're gonna meet us so we can make a plan of attack."

As the helicopter made its landing on the rooftop of their destination, Mugan turned to Slicer. "You'll get there quicker if I fly there direct. You mind hitching a ride with me?"

Slicer nodded, with an air of hesitation as he realized just what Mugan meant. "Don't mind me if my eyes are closed the whole time," he replied.

Mugan powered down the helicopter. As the rotors ground to a stop, the trio disembarked and walked toward the rooftop access door. Ife pulled out her identification badge and prepared to unlock the door. She turned to Mugan and Slicer. "Good luck, gents," she said. "Let's fix this."

Mugan and Slicer gave her a friendly, if hurried wave. Slicer hooked his arms around Mugan's waist and secured himself with a few carabiners. Mugan waited until Slicer was situated, then crouched and suddenly launched into the night sky, a blur of vampire speed and determination.

Hunter stumbled through the dimly lit halls of the medical lab, his hand pressed against the cold, damp wall for support. His breaths came in ragged gasps, the hallucinations clawing at the edges of his vision. He had stumbled through the break room and located two bottles of Evermore chilling in the fridge. He downed them quickly, and a short vomiting spell later, the poison pill had been expelled. But its effects still lingered, twisting his reality into a nightmarish landscape. The hall seemed to expand and contract like the bellows of an accordion as he staggered.

"Kate," he muttered under his breath, his voice hoarse. "Where are you?"

The sound of mocking laughter echoed through the halls, distant but unmistakable.

Kate? Hunter turned in place, the effort sending a wave of dizziness coursing through him.

No, it wasn't Kate's voice. It was his own.

"Looking for someone, Hunter?"

He froze, the hairs on the back of his neck standing on end. Slowly, he turned, and there it was–a shadowy figure leaning casually against the wall. It wasn't the oily black visage of a dark cloud this time. It was *him*, but not quite. The Hunter facing him now was gaunt, with hollow eyes and an unsettling grin that twisted his features into something cruel and unrecognizable.

"You're wasting your time," the hallucination said, pushing off the wall and circling him like a predator. "She's long gone, and so are *you*. So far gone."

Hunter clenched his fists, his nails biting into his palms. "You're not real."

The figure laughed, a harsh, grating sound that made Hunter's skin crawl. "Real enough to remind you of what a loser you are? You're chasing ghosts, stumbling around like a broken doll, thinking you can fix things."

Hunter forced himself to take a step forward, brushing past the hallucination. "Get out of my head."

But the shadowy figure reappeared in front of him, blocking his path. Its grin widened, revealing jagged teeth. "I'm not in your head, Hunter. I *am* your head. Every doubt, every failure, every mistake–you carry me with you, feeding me every time you falter."

Hunter's vision wavered, the walls seeming to bend and twist. The shadow leaned closer, its voice a whisper now, soft but relentless. "Just give up. It's easier. You're tired, Hunter. So tired. Why keep fighting when it would feel so much better to stop?"

"No!" Hunter shouted, his voice echoing down the hall. He swung his fist, and for a moment, the shadow flickered and dissipated like smoke.

His knuckles struck the wall instead, the pain grounding him in the moment. He leaned heavily against it, his chest heaving, sweat mingling with the cold air. The shadow didn't return, but its words lingered, echoing in his mind.

"You don't get to win," Hunter muttered to himself, his voice trembling but defiant. He pushed off the wall, forcing his legs to move. "Not today."

The hallway stretched on before him, dim and oppressive, but he kept going. Each step felt like a small victory, a refusal to let the darkness take hold.

The sound of his own footsteps echoed eerily in the cavernous space along with the mocking sounds of a woman's laughter. Outside, the snowstorm howled, a relentless force of nature that made escape seem even more impossible. He turned a corner and froze.

There, slumped against the wall, at the end of a broad arc of dark blood, was a lifeless body. Hunter was barely able to make out the face.

"Trevor," Hunter whispered, his voice filled with dread. He knelt beside the body, his trembling hand reaching out. As his fingers brushed Trevor's cold skin, a surge of energy coursed through him. His eyes and the eyes of Trevor's corpse flashed purple, pulling him into a psychic vision.

In the vision, Trevor stood in the same hallway, his steps hesitant as he approached Kate. Her back was to him, her shoulders rigid. When she turned, her eyes were black and empty, void of humanity. A guttural, demonic growl erupted from her lips, and she lunged at Trevor with unnatural speed. The vision shattered as quickly as it had come, leaving Hunter reeling.

He staggered to his feet, his head pounding. "Kate... you're a fucking demon?"

Driven by a mix of fear and determination, Hunter made his way through the labyrinthine halls, his steps quickening as the storm outside grew louder. He reached an exit and stepped into the blinding white chaos. The snow whipped against his face, the cold biting into his skin. He ignored the biting cold as snow and ice pellets bounced off his bare chest, ignored the flashing glow of the tribal tattoo as it sent out its beacon into the ether.

The landscape before him was a scene of desolation—bodies littered the snow, their blood stark against the blinding white. Some bore the unmistakable signs of claw and fang marks, others shredded beyond recognition. The storm blurred the edges of the carnage, but the evidence was clear.

Hunter trudged through the snow, the storm blurring the line between earth and sky. He was panting as a familiar rage washed over him, the fire-like burning within him causing visible puffs of warm air, his chest heaving with the effort of each step.

He came across a body half-buried in the snow, one arm stretched out as though the person had tried to crawl to safety. The sight churned his stomach, but he pressed on, crouching beside the lifeless figure. A young woman, her face pale and frozen in terror, stared up at him with unseeing eyes.

Swallowing hard, Hunter extended a trembling hand. His fingers brushed against her cold, stiff arm, and the familiar rush of power surged through him. His vision darkened, and the world shifted.

Suddenly, he was standing in her shoes.

She was running, her feet slipping on the ice-slicked ground. The storm whipped around her, snowflakes stinging her face. Behind her, a guttural snarl cut through the howling wind, sending a jolt of fear down her spine. She risked a glance back and saw her attacker, sprinting like a gazelle toward her.

"No, no, no," she whispered, her voice barely audible over the storm. She stumbled, falling to her knees, her breath hitching as the shadow of her pursuer loomed over her. She tried to scream, but a clawed hand gripped her throat, lifting her effortlessly off the ground.

The figure's face came into focus—a woman with black, empty eyes and a cruel smile. "No one escapes," *the demon growled, her voice like nails on glass.*

The last thing the young woman saw was the flash of claws slicing through the air.

Kate had gone on a rampage, a frenzy of violence and hunger left within her wake.

Hunter's stomach churned as he forced himself forward, each step sinking into the snow. The howling wind masked any sound of movement, leaving him feeling isolated and exposed. As he approached what he thought was solid ground, his foot broke through the surface. Ice. A thin, treacherous sheet concealed a gaping pit below. He plunged downward, the icy walls rushing past him as he fell into darkness.

18

FRIGID INFERNO

The frigid shock tore into Hunter like knives, his breath fleeing in a ragged gasp as he plunged beneath the surface. Water pressed against him from all sides, black and infinite, carrying him down into a freezing abyss. Instinct kicked in, and he clawed upward, only to slam his fists against a sheet of unyielding ice.

Panic surged, and Hunter thrashed wildly, searching for the hole he'd fallen through. The water churned with his movements, and though he didn't need to breathe, his mind betrayed him, falling back on human habits. The phantom sensation of his lungs screaming for air sent jolts of fear through his body, his chest tightening with every second he spent under the ice.

This was the dream. The nightmare that had haunted him since the beginning—the icy grip of death closing in, cold water stealing every shred of warmth. But this wasn't a dream. The pain in his limbs was too sharp, the cold too real.

A brilliant flash of light pierced the darkness, its intensity cutting through the icy gloom. For a moment, the water around him seemed to ripple with the aftershock of its arrival. Then, Gibson was there, his form shimmering faintly as if the light still clung to him.

"Hunter!" Gibson's voice was muffled and distorted by the water, but the urgency in it was unmistakable. He reached out, grasping Hunter's arm with a strength that steadied his younger partner's frantic movements.

Hunter gestured wildly upward, the universal sign of desperation. *Ice. Escape. Now.* Gibson nodded, his face set with determination. Together, they kicked into motion, their movements awkward but purposeful in the frigid water.

The expanse of ice above seemed endless, a cruel ceiling trapping them below. Hunter's thoughts spun as he searched for anything—a shadow, a fissure, a glimmer of light—that might lead them to an exit. Every second felt like an eternity as his body grew heavier, the cold leeching away what strength he had left.

Gibson pulled him sharply to the side, pointing toward a faint shimmer to their right. The light was dim, diffused through the ice, but it was hope. They swam toward it with everything they had, their movements frantic and uncoordinated. Hunter's vision blurred at the edges, the phantom need to be amid air making the world spin, but he kept moving. He had to. They both did.

When they reached the source of the light, Hunter's heart sank. It wasn't an opening, just a thin patch of ice where the sunlight filtered through. He slammed his fist against it in frustration, a muffled scream escaping his lips as bubbles rushed from his mouth.

Gibson's grip tightened on his arm as if trying to anchor Hunter to his body. Then, Gibson pointed behind Hunter. Turning, Hunter could see another clump of white ice, seeming to form a cavernous tunnel. Was this another potential way to move or was it what they had just swum out of? Hunter hesitated, his body instinctively rejecting the idea of swimming deeper into the freezing darkness. But Gibson's pointed look left no room for argument. *Trust me*, it seemed to say.

With what little strength remained, Hunter followed Gibson into the depths. They swam side by side, their movements synchronized now, driven by a shared will to survive. The water grew darker, colder, and Hunter's mind fought against the primal fear clawing at his thoughts.

And then they saw it—a faint glow, pulsating gently like a heartbeat. A crack in the ice, larger than the rest, with open water leading to the surface. Gibson motioned for Hunter to follow, his movements urgent but measured.

But as they neared the crack, the glow began to fade. The ice was thick, too thick to break with force alone. Hunter hesitated, his chest tightening as his mind raced. Then, with a resolve born of desperation, he clenched his fists and focused inward.

Heat began to build in his core, defying the freezing water that surrounded him. Fire. It was a power that shouldn't work here, submerged and surrounded by liquid. But it was his, a defiance of nature that he could control. His hands began to glow, a flicker of warmth spreading through his veins.

Gibson's eyes widened, and he gestured for Hunter to hurry. The crack above them was their only chance, and the ice wasn't going to wait.

Hunter thrust his hands upward, pressing them against the thick sheet of ice. A surge of heat burst from his palms, the water around them bubbling and steaming in a surreal display. The ice hissed and cracked, fractures spreading outward like veins of light. He pushed harder, pouring every ounce of his strength into the effort.

With a deafening crack, the ice gave way, a jagged opening forming above them. Light poured through, blinding but glorious. Hunter grabbed Gibson's arm, and together they propelled themselves upward, breaking the surface in a triumphant surge.

Hunter's hands broke through first, and then his head, gasping despite the lack of true need for air. His body instinctively sought comfort, dragging him onto the ice. The air was sharp and biting, but it was a mental balm, and he gulped it down greedily.

Gibson surfaced a moment later, heaving, expelling water from his lungs. He pulled himself out beside Hunter, the two of them collapsing on the ice, their bodies shivering uncontrollably.

Hunter's senses, sharpened by his part-demon nature, suddenly pricked at something unusual. Beneath the biting cold and the metallic tang of the ice, a scent lingered–faint but unmistakable. It was familiar in a way that made his pulse quicken. His alternate-world form.

"Where..." Hunter rasped, his voice hoarse from instinctive gasping. "Where is he? Where's the other Hunter?"

Gibson shook his head, his face pale and solemn. "I don't know," he said, his voice barely audible over the sound of the wind. "I didn't feel him with me when I hit the water."

Hunter's eyes darted around, his mind racing. The scent was faint, but it was there, carried on the cold air. Hunter II was nearby. Somewhere. And they had to find him.

The schooner's deck creaked under the weight of Slicer's heavy boots as he paced back and forth, his restless energy barely contained. The shapeshifting biker leader's crew moved around him with quiet efficiency while the snowstorm swirled around their forms, as the rising sun threatened to break the horizon. They were a pack, and their movements spoke of practiced unity, a fluid dance of loyalty and shared purpose.

Mugan had arrived just moments before, descending from the darkened sky with Slicer in his grasp. His vampiric ability to fly had made the journey swift and silent, a stark contrast to the tension now brewing aboard the ship. He had deposited Slicer onto the deck with a flick of his wrist, as if the man weighed nothing, before retreating below deck to avoid the coming sunlight.

As the schooner drifted closer to Matthew Island, the unnatural stillness in the air set everyone on edge. Slicer's sharp senses caught the telltale signs of something grim: the lack of movement along the distant shoreline, patches of dark stains on the rocks that glistened in the pale light–blood, unmistakably fresh. The scent of death hung heavy in the air among the snow, a cloying reminder that violence had swept through this place mere hours ago.

"Something's wrong," Slicer murmured, his voice low but carrying the weight of certainty. His crew stilled, their feral eyes scanning the horizon, their noses twitching as they caught the same scent. Whatever had happened here, it was recent, and it had been bloody.

Mugan, however, remained below deck. The approaching daylight was a death sentence for him if he dared to step above. He paced the narrow cabin like a caged animal, his pale skin nearly glowing in the dim lamplight. But his agitation was tempered by purpose. He had knowledge–of Matthew Island and the facility Kate Coupland had used as her refuge. It was information Slicer and his pack would need to get the job done.

Another figure emerged from below deck: Piston, the contact Slicer had called for reinforcements. A wiry man with an uncanny ability to blend into any crowd, Piston was a jack-of-all-trades, his expertise ranging from mechanical ingenuity to tactical planning. His sharp, dark eyes swept the deck before fixing on Slicer.

"Storm's going to make landing tricky," Piston said, his voice smooth but weighted with confidence. "But if we hit the southern cliffs, like Mugan said, I've got the tools to deal with any surprises that tunnel might throw our way."

Slicer gave a nod, clearly trusting Piston's judgment. "Good to have you on this, Piston. You brought everything we need?"

Piston smirked, tapping the duffel slung over his shoulder. "Explosives, cutting gear, and a few other toys. Just in case things get...complicated."

Slicer paused, his yellow-tinged eyes narrowing as he processed the information. He responded, his tone laced with appreciation, "Good to know. That'll save us some time."

He turned to his crew, his posture straightening with renewed focus. "Listen up," he growled, summoning them. "We're heading for the south cliffs. The terrain's rough, but it'll keep us hidden. From there, we'll use the tunnel Mugan mentioned to get inside. Quick and quiet, no exceptions."

One of the younger pack members, a wiry woman with a scar running from her temple to her jaw, leaned in. "We could use the storm cover to get closer. Looks like it's heading right over the south coast."

Slicer nodded, his fingers tracing the map spread out across a weathered table near the helm. "Good. We'll anchor here, just off the southern cliffs. Move fast and keep low."

Another voice cut in, deeper and edged with doubt. "And what about Mugan? He's not exactly stealthy."

"He's a vamp; he'll have stay here," Slicer said, his tone firm but lacking the edge of impatience. "We'll handle the approach. Once we locate Kate, we call him in for the kill."

Piston cleared his throat, drawing attention back to himself. "And what about Hunter? If he's out there, sunlight's going to be a problem. You know he won't last long without cover."

Slicer's expression darkened, a flicker of concern breaking through his otherwise stoic demeanor. "We've got the heavy blackout blankets and a spare UV-shield tarp. If we find him, we'll make sure he's protected." He paused, his voice softening just enough to betray the depth of his worry. "Hunter's one of us. We don't leave our own to burn."

Below deck, Mugan's acute hearing caught every word. He allowed himself a faint smile. Trust in his resourcefulness was well-placed, and he relished the role he played in orchestrating the coming strike. The pack could take point; he would be the blade that delivered the final blow.

The schooner rocked gently as the crew began their preparations, the rising sun painting the horizon in hues of gold and crimson. Slicer glanced at the lightening sky, his sharp features hardening. Time was running out, and they all knew it.

"Move fast," he barked, his voice cutting through the morning stillness. "We've got one chance to make this work. Let's not waste it."

Hunter and Gibson struggled not to yell out in frustration as the storm whirled around them, pelting their wet bodies with ice pellets and snow. Each bit felt like a pinprick against the skin, the sub-zero temperatures agonizing even for their dead, vampiric bodies.

"We-we've got to warm up and fast," Gibson shivered. "Wh-wh-where's the facility?" The uncharacteristic fear underlying his words startled Hunter.

"J-j-just ahead," Hunter said. Hesitating, he added, "I-I-I think."

Before they could proceed further, a figure emerged from the swirling snow, moving with purpose and urgency. Hunter's senses flared, and he caught the unmistakable scent of himself–and yet not. It was the scent of his alternate self, Hunter II.

"Inside," Hunter II commanded, his voice sharp and brooking no argument. "Now."

Hunter and Gibson scrambled to their feet, following the doppelgänger as he led them to a concealed entrance. The heavy metal door groaned as it swung open, revealing a narrow staircase that plunged into the depths of the facility. The moment they were inside, Hunter II slammed the door shut, sealing them in darkness save for the faint red glow emanating from his hands.

"Hold still," he ordered, his tone softer now. He raised his glowing palms, and a wave of warmth washed over Hunter and Gibson, chasing away the chill that had seeped into their bones. The frost clinging to their clothes melted away, replaced by a comforting heat that radiated from within.

Hunter studied his counterpart in the dim light. The similarities were uncanny, but there was a hardness in Hunter II's eyes that spoke of battles fought and losses endured. This was a man–a version of himself–who had seen some shit in his life. Just like he had.

"You've got questions," Hunter II said, his lips quirking into a wry smile. "But they'll have to wait. This place isn't safe, and we're not alone."

Gibson stepped forward, his jaw set. "Who else is here?"

Hunter II's nose pointed toward the facility like a bloodhound. "Kate. She'll have felt that little fireworks display you pulled."

"Kate?" Gibson shook his head in disbelief. "No way. Kate's been in Texas with Kai all this--"

He stopped himself too late. Hunter's expression of confusion, combined with his duplicate's stern, stoic face caught up with him.

"There are two Kates; just like there are two Hunters," the other-realm Hunter said, his voice calm but weighted. "But this version of Kate isn't just a duplicate. She's something else entirely. She is most definitely a *Greater Rakhion* -- I can smell it. A predator. She can tear through flesh like a piranha through water. I've seen what she's capable of."

"By the gods," Gibson muttered, his voice barely audible as he processed the revelation.

Hunter II's features hardened further. "I've been tracking her as part of my work as a Watcher for The Crown. She's dangerous, and she's been building strength here. This facility is hers now, and she won't let intruders go unnoticed."

Hunter tensed, his hands clenching as his ears were bombarded with even more new information. "Whoa, what, The Crown?"

Hunter II nodded, his tone grim. "Yes. The Crown thinks I'm a sovereign member of their group... just like this Kate *is*. And she knows we're here. And we don't have much time."

Gibson glanced between the two Hunters, his resolve sharpening. "Do we have a plan?"

"We survive," Hunter II said. "Follow me. I'll explain what I can on the way."

Without another word, he turned and descended deeper into the labyrinthine facility, his red glow illuminating the path ahead. Hunter and Gibson followed close behind, their senses heightened and their resolve steeled.d and their resolve steeled for whatever lay ahead.

The passageway curved downward, its walls smooth and featureless. The sterile atmosphere of the place was broken only by the distant hum of machinery. As they turned a corner, a sharp whistle cut through the air. Hunter's head snapped up, his heightened senses locking onto the sound.

"About time you showed up!"

The familiar voice of Slicer echoed through the corridor, and Hunter breathed an unnecessary sigh of relief. The leather-clad biker emerged from the shadows, flanked by his pack of shifters. Behind him stood Piston, his rugged build and piercing gaze exuding calm confidence.

"You made it," Hunter said, his voice thick with gratitude.

Slicer smirked. "You think we'd leave you to handle this mess on your own?"

Hunter II stepped out from behind his duplicate. Slicer's smirk dropped immediately. "What the actual fuck?"

"Long, long story," Hunter said.

"We're not out of this yet," Hunter II said. Kate's here. I think she's alone, based on what I can smell."

Slicer nodded. "We figured as much. The air's thick with death. It's been hours since anything alive moved out there. Except for us."

Hunter II glanced at Piston. "Do you have a way to protect everyone from her?"

Piston nodded. "We've got reinforced barriers and a few tricks up our sleeves. But we'll need to move fast. This place is a maze, and she knows it better than we do."

Slicer placed a hand on Hunter's shoulder. "And what about you, pup? You ready to face her?"

Hunter felt the weight of the question, but he nodded. "We don't have a choice."

Gibson stepped between them. "If she's half as dangerous as we've been told, we'll need a plan."

Hunter II's voice was firm. "We find her, neutralize her, and get out. But first, we stick together. Splitting up is suicide."

Piston gestured toward a side corridor. "There's a control room up ahead. It might give us the advantage we need. If we can lock down her movements—"

A sudden, guttural roar echoed through the facility, freezing them in their tracks. Hunter II's eyes burned with intensity. "She knows we're here. Let's move."

The group fell into formation, their footsteps echoing through the cold, metallic halls as they braced themselves for the confrontation ahead.

The cold bit into the team as they advanced through the maze of corridors within the facility. Frost clung to the walls, but the oppressive silence was more chilling than the air. Every step echoed ominously.

Hunter II led the way, his glowing hands providing just enough light to guide them. Slicer and his pack flanked him, their supernatural senses attuned to every shift in the air. Behind them, Piston brought up the rear, lugging a weapon that looked more like a small cannon than a gun. Its reinforced steel frame gleamed dully in the dim light, cables snaking across the barrel to an under-slung power cell that hummed faintly with contained energy. The muzzle bore scorch marks from countless test fires, and the etched grooves along the grip hinted at a maker's obsession with perfection."

This place reeks of death," Slicer repeated, his voice low but carrying.

"She's been feeding," Hunter II replied grimly. "Every kill makes her stronger."

Hunter exchanged a glance with Gibson, whose jaw was set in determination. "Are we sure this plan is going to work?"

Hunter II stopped at a junction, his gaze sweeping the corridor ahead. "It has to. If we don't stop her here, she'll escape, and we'll lose our only chance to contain her."

The team split into two groups, each assigned to flank Kate from different sides. Hunter and Gibson stayed with Hunter II, while Slicer, Piston, and the pack circled around to cut off any escape routes.

As they neared the main chamber, the air grew thick and foreboding. A low, guttural growl reverberated through the walls, setting every nerve on edge.

"She's close," Gibson murmured.

Hunter II raised a hand, signaling for silence. The door to the chamber loomed ahead, partially ajar. Beyond it, a faint red light pulsed rhythmically, accompanied by the wet, visceral sounds of flesh and bone.

Hunter II pushed the door open with deliberate care. Inside, the chamber was a grotesque tableau of carnage. The remains of the facility's personnel lay scattered, their blood pooling in congealed rivulets across the icy floor. At the center of the room stood Kate, her form shifting between human and demon. Her razor-sharp claws glinted in the unnatural light, and her eyes burned with malice.

"So, the hunters have come to hunt," Kate hissed, her voice a distorted amalgamation of tones.

"You're done, Kate," Hunter II said, stepping forward. His voice was steady, but there was a hard edge to it.

Kate's lips curled into a smile, her teeth unnaturally sharp. "I was hoping you'd come. I've been dying to see which of you tastes better."

With a snarl, she lunged.

Hunter reacted instinctively, unleashing a wave of ice that surged across the floor, freezing her mid-charge. Kate hissed, her body encased in frost, but the moment was fleeting. Her body began to morph, her skin tone dissipating as her shape grew into a more gelatinous form, speckled with blue and purple, like a bizarre glitter toy. With a burst of strength, she shattered the ice and darted toward him.

"Hunter!" Gibson shouted, leaping into the fray to intercept her.

As Kate slashed at Gibson, Hunter felt a sudden, sharp pain in his chest. His vision blurred, and the room around him twisted into an all-too-familiar nightmare. The specter of his depression materialized, its cold, mocking voice echoing in his mind.

"You can't save them," it sneered. "You couldn't save yourself."

Hunter staggered, clutching his head. His breaths came in ragged gasps, though he knew he didn't need air. The hallucination was stronger this time, its grip suffocating.

Kate's laughter cut through his torment, sharp and taunting. Her voice melded with that of the specter of depression and suicidal tendencies he had been hearing throughout the ordeal. "You feel it, don't you? My venom in your veins, feeding your doubts, your fears. You're *mine*, Hunter."

But something within him stirred—a defiance that burned hotter than her venom.

"No," Hunter growled, his voice low but resolute.

The fire within him surged to life, consuming the ice. Flames erupted from his hands, their light and heat cutting through the hallucination like a blade. The specter screamed as it dissolved, leaving Hunter gasping but focused.

He turned his attention back to Kate, who now regarded him with a mix of amusement and wariness.

"You're stronger than I thought," she admitted, her tone laced with mockery.

Hunter didn't reply. He thrust his hands forward, unleashing a torrent of fire and ice in tandem. The opposing elements spiraled together, their combined force striking Kate with explosive power.

She shrieked, her form flickering as the attack overwhelmed her. Slicer's pack charged in, taking advantage of her weakened state to drive her toward the chamber's center.

From the shadows, Mugan emerged, cloaked in a protective tarp Slicer's crew had lent him. His presence was almost imperceptible until he stepped into the pulsing light. He moved with a predatory grace, his golden eyes locked onto Kate. In his hand, he withdrew the item sheathed by his hip: a blade forged from bone, its surface etched with runes that glowed faintly.

"Mugan!" Gibson called out, startled. "What are you..."

Mugan raised a hand, silencing him. "Stay back."

Kate turned to face him, her predatory grin faltering for the first time. "The Estinal," she growled, her voice laced with recognition and fear.

Kate let out a feral scream, her demonic form fully unleashed—a grotesque yet awe-inspiring figure of sinewy muscle, color-flecked gel, jagged horns, and smoldering crimson eyes that seemed to pierce the soul. Her claws, wickedly sharp and dripping with dark energy, lashed out as she charged, her movements a blur of fury and desperation.

But Mugan was faster. He sidestepped with inhuman precision, his body a streak of motion. The Estinal hummed, its blessed blade thrumming with ancient power, as it arced through the air and plunged into her chest. The impact was devastating.

Kate froze, her eyes widening in shock and pain as the blade's glowing runes ignited. They flared to life, golden light spiraling out like cracks in her skin, searing through her flesh with divine intensity. Her convulsions were violent, her body jerking as if fighting to reject the weapon's sacred energy.

"No!" she shrieked, her voice layered with distortion, an unearthly wail that reverberated through the chamber like the echo of a thousand damned souls. The oppressive energy she radiated swirled chaotically, tearing at the air as the room shuddered.

The runes pulsed brighter, drawing out dark tendrils of energy from within her, each strand unraveling her being. The scent of sulfur and charred flesh filled the air, acrid and heavy. Her once-mighty form began to crumble, cracks spreading across her body like a fragile porcelain shell under too much pressure.

"Caeden..." she gasped, her voice human for a fleeting moment—a final whisper of the person she once was before the corruption took hold.

Hunter, puzzled, wondered silently to himself: *Did she say 'Caeden?' Kai's old name?*

Then, the energy collapsed inward, a vortex of light and shadow consuming her. Her body disintegrated into ash, the remnants swirling momentarily before dissipating into nothingness. The oppressive weight in the room lifted, leaving an eerie stillness in its wake, broken only by the faint hum of The Estinal's blade.

Mugan stood over the remains, his face a blank, unreadable canvas. He turned to the others, his voice calm but resolute. "It's done."

Hunter, still catching his breath, felt the venom's effects recede, the burning doubt it had sown fading with Kate's death.

Without waiting for a response, Mugan strode out of the chamber, leaving the group to process what had just transpired.

Hunter broke the silence, his voice strained. "So...what's next?"

Gibson exhaled sharply, rubbing his temple. "We regroup. There's more you need to know, Hunter. About Calhoun, about Kai..."

Hunter's chest tightened. "What happened?"

His other-world duplicate stepped forward. His stoic features defied his punk-colored hair, his tone steady but grave. "Calhoun's dead, and Kai's been framed for it. This goes deeper than any of you first thought. Kate wasn't acting alone."

Slicer frowned, his voice laced with frustration. "Great. Another tangled web to unravel."

Hunter looked around the room, at the faces of his allies, and felt the weight of the fight ahead.

Kai sat on the edge of the bed in the dimly lit hotel room, his head in his hands. The pale light of the moon filtered through the lace curtains, casting long shadows on the pale cream wallpaper. His mind raced with the whirlwind of recent events: Calhoun's murder, the so-called evidence pinning the crime on him, and all the while, Hunter laying on the brink of who-knows what fate as his body decided just what kind of demon he was supposed to be .

A sharp knock at the door jolted him from his thoughts.

"Kai, it's Noah. Open up."

Kai opened the door a crack, peering out to confirm it was Noah before letting him in.

"What are you doing here?" Kai asked.

Noah stepped inside, his battered leather satchel slung over his shoulder. He glanced around the room before setting the bag down. "I'm here because you're in deep trouble, and I don't think you understand just how deep. Someone went to a lot of trouble to frame you, Kai. And I think I know who."

Kai frowned, his stomach tightening. "Who?"

Noah opened his satchel and pulled out a thin folder. "Take a look at this."

Kai flipped it open. Inside were photos–grainy surveillance images of Kate Coupland. But something was off. In one set of photos, she wore her hair differently and had an air of poise that was almost regal. In another set, she seemed rougher around the edges, her nose slightly more pointed, her smile more calculating.

Kai looked up at Noah, his confusion clear. "These... these are two different people. But it's Kate."

"Exactly," Noah said. "There are two of her. One here, in this alternate world, and one back in yours. I think both of them may be working for The Crown."

Kai stared at the photos, struggling to process the revelation. "How is this even possible?"

Noah shrugged. "Alternate dimensions, doppelgängers–thanks to Hunter, we know it's not unheard of anymore. But this? This is deliberate. They've been coordinating, using their similarities to infiltrate both worlds."

Kai clenched his fists, the weight of betrayal heavy in his chest. "Why would she do this? Why would *they* do this?"

Noah leaned forward, his voice low and urgent. "Think about it. Taking out Calhoun, the head of the largest ward in The Order destabilizes it. Blaming you shifts the focus. Meanwhile, the other Kate is working her way through Hunter's world, dismantling your allies from the inside." Kai slammed the folder shut, his jaw tight. "She's been playing us all this whole time."

Noah hesitated. "You've got to be smart about this."

Kai turned away, his mind racing. "What do we do?"

Noah pulled another folder from his satchel and set it on the table. "I honestly don't know yet. Everything is so fractured. But one thing's certain - you can't return to the home realm—not yet."

Kai spun to face him, his frustration clear. "Why not? She's operating in both worlds. I need to confront her—both of them—and get to the bottom of this."

Noah shook his head. "You're still the prime suspect in Calhoun's murder! If you go back, you'll be terminated on the spot -- I'm sure there's already a scroll out with your name on it. The Order won't give you the time to explain."

Kai's fists clenched, his shoulders tense. "So what, I just sit here while she continues her games?"

"No," Noah said firmly. "We focus on clearing your name and exposing her. Or *them*. Until then, you stay put. It's safer for you here than anywhere else."

Kai's chest heaved as he fought against his rising frustration. "And Hunter? Gibson? Are they safe? Do you even know where they are?"

Noah's face softened, his voice steady. "I don't know their exact location, but they've always been resourceful and I'm sure they're together. Trust me, Kai, the best thing you can do is stay alive and out of The Order's immediate reach. We'll figure out how to bring everyone back together when the time is right."

Kai sank back onto the bed, running a hand through his hair. "I hate this. Sitting on the sidelines while everyone else is in danger."

Noah placed a hand on his shoulder. "You're not sitting on the sidelines. You're surviving. And you're giving us the time we need to take this conspiracy apart. We'll find a way to make this right. I promise."

Kai exhaled slowly, the tension in his body easing slightly. "Fine. I'll stay. But the second you find something solid, you tell me."

Noah nodded. "You have my word."

19
ACCUSED

The rail yard stretched out before Caeden like a vast iron maze, the tracks gleaming faintly in the moonlight. Overhead, the stars glittered in a cloudless sky, their light pale and weak compared to the lanterns strung sporadically along the perimeter. The yard was mostly deserted at this hour, save for the occasional clink of metal or the distant hiss of steam escaping a dormant engine.

Caeden moved silently among the shadows, his footsteps muffled by the layers of gravel and earth beneath the rails. His sharp senses were attuned to every sound, every shift in the wind. The faint scent of oil and rust filled the air, mingling with something more subtle, something acrid and metallic that set his instincts on edge.

The west yard was his destination—the place Old Billy had mentioned. It was tucked farther from the central depot, an area used for less urgent freight. The sparse lighting here only deepened the shadows, making it the perfect spot for illicit activity or concealment.

As Caeden approached, his keen eyes scanned the ground for anything unusual. Discarded tools, scraps of metal, and old crates littered the area. Nothing out of place—yet. He moved carefully between the rows of rail cars, his senses stretching outward.

Then he saw it: a dark stain on the gravel near one of the older cars. Kneeling, Caeden examined the spot. The color was too deep for oil. He touched a finger to it, bringing it closer to his nose. Blood. Faint but undeniable. His jaw tightened, and his gaze swept the area for more clues.

Nearby, a faint glint caught his eye. Half-buried in the gravel was a small, thin object. He retrieved it and held it up to the moonlight. A button, tarnished and worn, with a faint engraving barely visible on its surface. He rubbed away some of the grime to reveal the initials "M.H." etched into the metal.

Slipping the button into his pocket, Caeden's mind raced. M.H. Could it be Milton Hargrove, the quiet boarder at Mrs. Howe's? Or was the engraving meant to mislead? The possibility of another name lingered, the ambiguity gnawing at him.

His focus sharpened as a faint sound reached his ears: heavy footfalls, deliberate and slow, echoing faintly from the far end of the yard. He straightened, blending into the shadows as his eyes tracked the movement. A figure emerged, tall and broad-shouldered, wearing a wide-brimmed hat. The man from Grossman's.

Caeden froze, his instincts flaring. The man carried something in his hand, glinting faintly in the lantern light. A knife? A tool? Whatever it was, it added weight to his already growing suspicion.

The man paused, looking around as though sensing he wasn't alone. Caeden held his breath, his stillness absolute. Moments passed, and the man eventually turned, walking toward a derelict freight car. He stepped inside, vanishing from view.

Caeden waited a long moment before retreating. Taking a shortcut back to town, he slipped into a heavily wooded area bordering the outskirts. The trees loomed tall and close, their branches intertwined to form a canopy that blocked out most of the moonlight. The scent of pine and damp earth filled his senses, but his thoughts were elsewhere.

The memory of the newspaper clipping crept back into his mind. The description of the Railroad Ripper's victims—their mutilated faces, the jagged blade wounds—triggered something deep within him. His fingers brushed against the button in his pocket, a tactile reminder of the investigation, but it did little to quiet the gnawing hunger stirring in his chest.

The urge to feed was becoming harder to ignore. He felt the faint sting of his fangs pressing against his gums, an unwelcome reminder of his nature. Caeden clenched his jaw and forced the hunger down, focusing on the rhythmic crunch of his boots on the forest floor. He'd fed recently enough to stave off weakness, but the bloody imagery had awakened a primal part of him he preferred to keep buried.

"Not now," he murmured to himself, his voice low and firm. The trees began to thin as he neared the edge of the forest. Beyond the shadows, the dim lights of Austin's town square came into view. The streets were quieter now, most shops closed for the night. A few late-night stragglers lingered near the saloon, their voices carrying faintly on the breeze:

"I heard he has scars up and down his arms, from dragging his own blade across hisself!"

"Well, *I* heard he's always dressed in a black cape so he can do his dirty deeds in alleyways."

"Even in broad daylight?"

"Mmhm, shadowy alleyways, of course."

"Now, how can that be? The papers say he always strikes at night."

"I hear the victims are ladies of the night."

"I heard the victims are all colored girls."

"Cain't they be both?"

"That's a bunch of bunk, Sis. That last girl, back in San Antone? She weren't colored. Well... no color 'cept *red*."

"Oh! What a vile thing to say. Watch your mouth or I'll take you down to Mother's and she'll give you a good soaping!"

A stray dog trotted across the square, its tail wagging lazily as it sniffed at an overturned barrel. Caeden stepped onto the cobblestone road, his presence unremarkable amid the dwindling activity.

He was reminded of an item he needed to buy back at Grossman's, and made a beeline for the store. As he pushed past the door, he saw a man in a ten-gallon hat and a brown uniform speaking to Grossman and an assembled group of customers. The man had a badge upon which the name 'Betz' was engraved.

"The Texas Rangers are quite up in arms over this last killing over in San Antone," Sheriff Betz said. "Apparently there have been deaths all up and down the Union Pacific line, and there hasn't been a rhyme or reason to it.

"The Rangers, therefore, are asking towns along the train path to institute a curfew to ensure the citizenry don't come into contact with this man, whoever he is."

A fist slammed onto the counter. "Damn!" The volume, along with the mild profanity, emitted a scandalized gasp from the few women present in the shop, as the gravelly-voiced man complained, "It's already past eight and I haven't found a bed yet."

The sheriff took an annoyed look at the man, who dabbed at his forehead with a black handkerchief. "And you are…?"

"Hitchens. Douglas Hitchens."

"Room and board shouldn't be an issue, Mr. Hitchens," said Sheriff Betz. "Mrs. Howe's is a fine establishment, and it's just up the road from" –

"Oh, pardon me, Sheriff," Caeden spoke up politely. "I'm afraid the couple Mrs. Howe lent the main room to decided to stay on a few more days. We're still full up there."

Hitchens snorted in reply. "I ain't looking for anything in the low-rent district anyways. I can spend a dollar or so on more comfortable accommodation."

The response caused Caeden to wrinkle his nose in mild disdain. He noticed a similar reaction on the sheriff's face.

"The Stephen F. Austin is about a mile from here," Betz said calmly. "If you start off now, you'll be there with time to spare for the curfew."

Grabbing his box of snuff from the shop counter, Hitchens made a beeline for the door. "Very well then," he said. "Evening." With a jangle of the bell, he was gone.

"Oh, Sheriff," said Grossman, "but do I need to appeal to you for a special exception for young Caeden here? He's my night watchman, you see, and, well, we do have those early morning deliveries."

Betz took a step backward and looked in Caeden's direction, seemingly looking him over for size. Removing his hat entirely, the sheriff scratched a balding spot on the top of his head. "As long as I'm aware about it, I don't think we need to put anything on paper. I'll make sure anyone who swings by here on their rounds knows about you."

Stepping forward, Betz narrowed one of his eyes and said to Caeden, "You just make sure you're either in here stocking those shelves or walking straight from here to the train depot and back again. Y'hear?"

Caeden was sure the sheriff wasn't intending to sound threatening, just telling him how it was. He nodded respectfully. "Yes, sir."

"But you won't need to start checking up on him 'til tomorrow," Grossman said, putting his spectacles back on his nose and checking over his register. "Tonight's the young man's night off. I reckon he'll be heading back to Mrs. Howe's once he leaves here."

"Very good. Well, I have a few more stops to make. Have a safe evening, y'hear?" Betz replaced the hat on his head, tipped it to the women in the room, and spun on his spurred heels and left.

"Now, young Caeden," Grossman said. "What brings you in here on your day off?"

"I need some soap, actually," he replied. "Mrs. Howe doesn't stock any for her guests."

By ten p.m., Grossman bid Caeden good night and escorted him out the front door of the shop, locking the door quickly behind him. Caeden made a point of walking deliberately in the direction of the boarding house, his head erect and his eyes alert. Even though he didn't feel any reason to worry about his own safety, Caeden remembered the sheriff warning everybody to pay attention to their surroundings.

The famed, ever-changing Texas weather was remaining true to its legend: Just two nights ago, the blazing sun had left the night air heavy with heat and humidity. Now, a cold north wind had blown into town, creating a series of rustles waving through the trees and directly into Caeden's face as he walked.

Caeden rubbed his hands over his bare arms. Despite having a vampire's body temperature, the stark change in the wind against his skin caused goose pimples to form. He rather liked the sensation – a faint reminder of some of the simple things about human life that came up from time to time.

Rain began to fall gently, first a drop or two, and then sheets upon sheets. Human or not, walking in the rain with a cold wind at your face could make anyone feel miserable. He picked up a short jogging pace as he continued on toward the boarding house.

He made it to the small farmhouse next to the boarding house. He remembered Mrs. Howe saying that there were extra oil lamps that could be used for heating when the need arose. She left him a key to the padlock so he could get his own materials without disturbing her.

Fumbling briefly for the key, he unlocked the padlock and made his way into the barn, starting up the steps to the hayloft. Near the top of the stairs was a cot. Caeden decided he'd sit for a few minutes to rest and maybe enjoy the sights and sounds of the rain as it pelted the barn. The squeaking of the cot springs were quickly muffled by a gale of wind creating a howl throughout the barn. Higher up, the wind was colder, even as it sluiced through the slight gaps in the wooden planks comprising the walls, needling the skin.

There was a cupboard in the loft area, housing a small supply of liniments and first aid materials for the horses. Caeden searched behind its doors hoping to find a blanket or two to dry himself on. Finding none, he decided to damn the storm and run back into the house as quickly as he could.

He bolted down the stairs and quickly exited the barn, being sure to lock the door back, then charged for the back door of the house, which led into the kitchen area. Caeden didn't have a key to this door; he reckoned he would have to knock loudly on the door, and risk disturbing everyone inside.

Caeden made one loud *thump* against the door, and was surprised to find the force of the impact caused the door to creak open. He poked his head inside. "Mrs. Howe?" He adjusted his eyes to the dim light from the one oil lamp lit inside the kitchen.

A sudden clap of thunder from the growing storm almost masked the sound of another door slamming shut. Vampire-assisted hearing let Caeden know it was the door to the front parlor closing. He could even hear footsteps scurrying away from the building.

Sensing something was terribly wrong, Caeden's fangs descended in self-defense. With slow, purposeful steps, Caeden crossed from the kitchen into the front parlor.

There, in front of the blazing fireplace, was the body of Mrs. Howe, face-down, a pool of blood rapidly growing underneath her head.

Caeden raced to the body and knelt down, turning it over, and recoiled at what he observed. A knife had quite obviously been rammed into her throat and jerked away, creating a horrible gash in the windpipe. There were also several cuts across her neck and against her cheek, as if the knife had been swiped again and again without regard to where the blows would land.

Mrs. Howe's eyes had also been slashed, creating a dark red waterfall to pour out over her face.

"Who goes there?!"

The shout from upstairs startled Caeden. He remained standing over Mrs. Howe's body, even as his brain told him to flee, even as he heard two pairs of footsteps charging downward from the staircase. All he could will himself to do was hide his fangs. He slapped a hand against his mouth to ensure they were gone... and managed to paint his face with Mrs. Howe's blood.

The couple who were renting the upstairs room now stood in horror at the bottom of the staircase, seeing the mutilated body of their landlady on the floor, and a young man standing over the corpse, covered in the victim's blood.

By the time Sheriff Betz arrived, the storm had intensified, lashing rain against the windows and filling the boarding house with the mournful howls of wind. The sheriff, a tall man with a commanding presence and sharp green eyes, entered the parlor, his heavy boots leaving muddy prints on the wooden floor. He took one look at Caeden, blood-streaked and standing stiffly near Mrs. Howe's body, and let out a sharp sigh.

"Well, I suppose I shouldn't be surprised," Betz muttered, pulling a handkerchief from his coat pocket to dab at his wet face. "Another grisly scene, and wouldn't you know, someone's standing right in the thick of it."

Caeden didn't flinch under the sheriff's scrutiny. His expression was calm, almost detached, though his mind raced with thoughts of how to explain himself without giving away anything about his vampiric nature or the real reason for his presence in town.

"It's not what it looks like," Caeden said evenly. "I heard something from the barn and came to check. The door was ajar, and then I found her like this."

"Convenient," Betz replied dryly. He crouched to examine the body, his brow furrowing at the savage cuts.

"Looks like our Ripper's handiwork. Or someone with a damn strong stomach."

"I'm telling the truth," Caeden insisted, keeping his tone steady. "I saw someone leaving through the front parlor door as I entered the kitchen. Whoever it was, they ran off before I could get a clear look."

"Mm-hmm." Betz straightened, fixing Caeden with a piercing gaze. "And what's this, then?" He motioned to Caeden's bloodied hands and face.

"I tried to see if she was still alive," Caeden explained. "I turned her over to check. That's how the blood got on me."

"Sure," Betz said, unconvinced. He turned to the couple who had come downstairs, both pale and wide-eyed. "You two saw him standing over her?"

"Yes, Sheriff," the man stammered. "Covered in blood, just like he is now."

"Anything else?" Betz asked, his tone sharp.

The woman hesitated, clutching her husband's arm. Her auburn hair tumbled over her shoulders as she spoke. "He... he had thrust his hand in his jacket pocket when we came down. Like he was hiding something."

Betz narrowed his eyes at Caeden. "Hiding something, were you?"

Caeden shook his head. "No. I–"

"Save it." Betz raised a hand to cut him off. "Turn out your pockets."

Caeden reached into his jacket pockets. He flinched when his right hand hit something cold and metallic that he did not recognize.

"And what's this?" Betz noticed the reaction and reached into Caeden's coat pocket, pulling out a small item: a knife, its blade slick with fresh blood.

Caeden's eyes widened. "That's not mine," he said quickly. "Someone must have planted it on me."

Betz held up the blade, inspecting it under the flickering firelight. The craftsmanship was intricate but unremarkable–functional rather than decorative. "A hell of a coincidence, you being here and this being on you. Not to mention the bloody mess you're wearing."

"Sheriff, I swear–"

Betz sighed and motioned for his deputy, who had entered quietly behind him. "Get the cuffs on him. I don't like coincidences."

"You're making a mistake," Caeden said, his voice steady but firm. "I didn't kill her."

"Maybe you didn't," Betz replied, his tone clipped. "But you're looking mighty suspicious right now, and until we sort this out, you're coming with me. Deputy Harris, you stay here and wait for the doc to come collect the body."

As Caeden was led out into the storm, he cast one last glance back at the parlor. His sharp eyes scanned the room, lingering on the faintest trail of muddy footprints leading away from the front door–proof of someone else's hurried escape.

None of them – not Caeden, not the sheriff, nor the deputy – could see, through the driving rain and wind, a man standing behind a tree just across the road from Howe's Boarding House. The man watched as Caeden was loaded into the black carriage with barred windows.

He watched as the sheriff climbed into the driver's seat of the coach and drove away.

Seeing it safely off into the distance, the man stepped out from under the tree and smiled. A flash of lightning spilled across the sky from above, revealing the man looked quite a lot like Caeden – virtually identical, in fact, if not five or six years' older in appearance.

His tight-lipped smile faded slightly when he heard a female voice calling to him. He turned to see the auburn-haired woman from Mrs. Howe's run across the street.

"You'll catch your death of cold coming out here like that," he said calmly.

"Never mind that," she said. She pushed her fingers into the skin of her face, which shifted like clay being repositioned to make a new sculpture. A clear gelatin-like mold formed into human-like skin. When the transformation was finished, this woman looked completely different. "Do you think this will be enough to take him out of the picture?"

"Time will tell," the man replied.

"What do I need to do in the meantime?"

"Go back into the house," he replied. "Keep up with the story. You and your 'husband' need to keep up the visage of a couple who witnessed Caeden Taylor commit a terrible crime. But don't embellish too much. We turn the screws on him little by little, and I'm sure he will crack."

"Yes, Mr. Taylor," the woman replied.

"Good work, Katherine," Caeden Taylor IV said. "Keep it up."

Smiling, Katherine Coupland nodded reverently, then trotted her way back across the street and into the boarding house.

This story will continue in
Bloodbound #5: Reverberations.

www.ingramcontent.com/pod-product-compliance
Ingram Content Group UK Ltd.
Pitfield, Milton Keynes, MK11 3LW, UK
UKHW022123110325
456116UK00009B/186